The Shy Stegosaurus
of Cricket Creek

By EVELYN SIBLEY LAMPMAN

Illustrated by Hubert Buel

SCHOLASTIC **SBS** BOOK SERVICES

Published by Scholastic Book Services, a division
of Scholastic Magazines, Inc., New York, N. Y.

To
Peggy and Naomi
who like dinosaurs

Copyright © 1955 by Evelyn Sibley Lampman. This edition is
published by Scholastic Book Services, a division of Scholastic
Magazine, Inc., by arrangement with Doubleday & Company, Inc.

4th printing .... April 1967

Printed in the U.S.A.

Chapter One

"JOEY! JOAN! The professor's forgotten his lunch again. You'll have to harness up Daisy Belle and take it to him."

Mrs. Brown opened the back door a small crack to call. Heat pushed against her face eagerly, and she stepped outside, closing the door behind her. She just couldn't seem to get used to this weather. At this time of day, when there was no breeze, it was wisdom to keep the doors and windows tightly closed. It kept what cool air there was inside and warm air out.

Down by the long-unused corral she caught a glimpse of faded blue, strangely out of place against the pounded brown of the earth. Blue was one of nature's colors reserved solely for the sky above Cricket Creek and the surrounding countryside, so she stepped to the edge of the porch and called again.

"Joey! Joan!"

The splotches of faded blue seemed to grow larger as Joey and Joan, who had been crouched in absorption over something on the ground, stood up. The children were dressed alike in much-washed blue jeans and cotton shirts. On their heads they wore large straw hats. One of them waved to Mrs. Brown enthusiastically.

"We found a funny bug, Mom. When you poke it, it curls up and rolls."

"Better leave it," called Mrs. Brown, shading her eyes from the glare. "The professor forgot his lunch."

Instantly both of the blue-clad figures began running toward the house. They were evenly matched, and the race ended in a tie.

"Mercy," said Mrs. Brown in alarm. "I should think you'd get a sunstroke, tearing around that way in all this heat."

"What heat?" demanded Joey in surprise. "It's been lots hotter than this. This is a pretty nice day."

"Did the professor really forget his lunch again, Mom?" asked Joan, beaming with delight. "He's just like the professors you read about, isn't he? Absentminded. I'm glad he's that way."

"I'm not," said Mrs. Brown, shooing them before her into the house and closing the door quickly behind her. "He's a nice man, and I'm thankful for his board money, but he's a great responsibility. He's so thin now that you'd think a hard wind would blow him away, yet when he forgets his lunch, as he's forever doing, he won't take time to come back after it."

"What he's doing is important," Joan told her wisely. "He's looking for dinosaur bones."

"It's important to us too," Joey added quickly. "Because, don't forget, if he finds them on our land he says he'll pay us money for them."

"Bones!" said Mrs. Brown wearily. "The only bones he's likely to find around here are those of some old cow that got caught in a winter blizzard, or maybe a coyote that somebody took a pot shot at."

The twins regarded their mother with round blue eyes in troubled faces. They were amazingly alike, despite the difference in their sex. Both had red hair, although Joey's was cut shorter than his sister's. Both had small upturned noses, covered with freckles, and wide mouths which generally turned upward at the corners. Their mouths were not smiling now. They were straight and drooped ever so slightly as they remembered the family Problem.

Joan was the first to put it from her mind.

"If we're going to take the professor his lunch, we'd better get going," she said brightly. "It's close to three miles, and Daisy Belle doesn't go very fast."

"It's there on the table." Mrs. Brown nodded. "And after this, let's all of us watch to make sure he doesn't forget again. I hate to have you riding in this heat."

"We'd be out in it anyway, Mom," said Joey reasonably. "So we might as well be riding as not."

They got the tin lunch pail from the kitchen table and went back to the barnyard where Joey put a blanket, in lieu of a saddle, on Daisy Belle, slipped the bit into her mouth, and led her over to the fence where it was easier to climb on.

"If we *do* have to go back to town," said Joan, suddenly returning to the Problem, "what would happen to Daisy Belle? We couldn't take her with us."

"Why couldn't we?" demanded Joey loudly.

"They don't allow horses in town. You know that. Besides, she belongs here. She was here when we came. I expect she's always lived here."

"I guess she has," agreed Joey.

He suddenly remembered the day, only three months ago, when the truck had brought them and their household goods to the ranch on Cricket Creek. They had expected so much of the ranch before they got here. It had seemed like something out of a fairy tale the day the lawyer had told Mom her Great-uncle Henry had left it to her. A ranch of their own! Mom could quit her job. Mrs. Hedgepeth, the cross housekeeper, wouldn't come any more, for if they lived on a ranch there would be enough money for Mom to stay home. They'd get a cow and chickens, and grow their own vegetables, and have horses!

Joey looked around the barnyard with disillusioned eyes. The ranch house was in a little valley between two hills, the unpainted buildings and fences weathered gray and seeming to sag noticeably from their yearly strain against the winter's storms. Cricket Creek threaded a sad, dry path of saffron dust across one side of the ravine, for at this time of year it was a creek in name only. Between the barn and the house, a vegetable garden panted under the sun, the growth wilted and stunted

4

despite the many buckets of water which the twins carried daily from the well. A solitary chicken, all that remained after a coyote had raided the chicken house one night, clucked and scratched across Joey's line of vision, and he scowled even harder.

"Come on," ordered Joan. "Daisy Belle can't stand here all day."

He climbed up in front of his sister and took the reins.

"Get up, Daisy Belle," he commanded affectionately.

Good old Daisy Belle! She had been the only one there to greet them when they arrived. Old and considered worthless by everyone else, she had been overlooked when the other horses were sold to pay for Great-uncle Henry's funeral. The twins had found her patiently waiting for someone to open the barn door, and they had adopted each other immediately.

Daisy Belle plodded slowly, panting already, for the climb was steep. Abrupt slopes dropped down into the valley — brown, dry, dotted with sagebrush. Once they reached the top, rolling plains spread roughly before them, but hemmed in, even on this higher level, by rim-rock cliffs to the north and south. A gravel road cut through the desertlike expanse, running from east to west, but after following it a little way Joey turned Daisy Belle to the left.

"Tire marks going off here," he said wisely. "The professor will be digging over against that cliff most likely."

"You don't mean digging," Joan reminded him. "He doesn't use a shovel."

5

"He will if he finds a really big one," insisted Joey. "I asked him. And I hope he does find a big one. I hope he finds the biggest whopper of a dinosaur anybody's ever found yet. We need the money."

"I know," sighed Joan. "But even if he doesn't find any, his board helps a little."

It had seemed like a second miracle the day Professor Harris had driven his car into the yard and inquired if they had any objections to his searching for bones of prehistoric animals on their land. Mrs. Brown had said no indeed, go right ahead, and Joey had asked curiously, "What do you want with old bones?"

"If I find anything worthwhile it will go to the museum," answered Professor Harris, smiling.

"Are they very valuable?"

"Oh, yes."

"Then if you find them on our land, they belong to us," said Joey quickly.

"Why, Joey," said Mrs. Brown in embarrassment, but he pretended not to hear.

The ranch hadn't brought them what they expected, but perhaps they hadn't expected the right thing. Now that he and Joan were twelve, Joey was beginning to understand about money. Money, or the lack of it, was their Problem. The arid ranch wouldn't support them, after all. Mrs. Brown's small widow's pension wouldn't cover food and clothing too. There was a reserve of five hundred dollars hidden away in an empty cookie jar, but Mrs. Brown had explained that five hundred dollars wasn't as much as it seemed. It wouldn't last any time at all if one of them got sick. Besides, there were such things as dentist bills, schoolbooks, and taxes which must be paid for somehow.

"Certainly they're yours," agreed the professor. "And if my theory is right, and I find what I'm looking for, I'll see that you're paid for them."

"Oh, Joey," said Mrs. Brown again.

"Not at all," smiled the professor. "The boy is right. And there is a fund for that purpose. Of course, I may be wrong. I may find nothing at all. But the formation, the sedimentary rock, the country itself — everything points to evidence that dinosaurs were once here in abundance."

"Where will you dig?" demanded Joan curiously. "May we watch you?"

"Now you children mustn't make a nuisance of your-selves," said Mrs. Brown hurriedly.

"They won't bother me at all," insisted the professor. "I thought I'd start on that rock formation to the left. Those cliffs a couple of miles from here. I'll pitch a camp and work out from there."

"Oh, my!" exclaimed Mrs. Brown. "It's so hot there. No shade at all."

"And no water," added Joey. "You'll have to come back here every day to get your water."

"You wouldn't mind?"

"You're welcome to all the water you need," said Mrs.

Brown quickly, "for drinking, and cooking, and washing your clothes. The next ranch is a long stretch down the road. Ours will be the closest. It's only a couple of miles, as you say, from the cliff you're talking about."

"Hm," said the professor thoughtfully. Instead of thanking her for her invitation to make use of the well, he seemed to be absorbed with a thought which had just come to him.

"I wonder," he began haltingly, "if you would consider taking me in as a boarder while I am here? Since I will have to drive this far for water anyway, it would be a great convenience. I wouldn't have to cook for myself. I'm a miserable cook."

"Well — " Mrs. Brown hesitated, and both twins turned to her eagerly.

"Sure, Mom," cried Joey. "He can have my room."

"And I'll help with the extra work," offered Joan.

"Oh, I wouldn't need to take your room," put in the professor hastily. "I have a tent. I'd only need breakfasts and dinners."

"You'd need a lunch," said Mrs. Brown, glancing at the professor's thin, almost gaunt, frame. "I'd pack you a lunch. It's too long to go between meals otherwise."

And that's how Professor Harris came to the ranch on Cricket Creek as a boarder. His compact little tent was pitched on the shadiest side of the house, and his old car chugged slowly up the steep slope early every morning and returned a little after dusk each night. His board money was added each week to the sum already in the

8

cookie jar, and for the time being Mrs. Brown said no more about the family's returning to town.

Since it was not the first occasion on which the professor had forgotten his lunch and the twins had been sent to deliver it, they knew where to look. They saw him from a distance, a small figure which grew larger as they approached. He was climbing up and down the face of the cliff, moving slowly, and searching the deep-cut gullies on the surface.

"I should think he'd find a dinosaur bone there if there was one to be found," said Joan thoughtfully. "I'm sure he would."

"Why?" demanded Joey.

"Because all those funny rocks look like they ought to be dinosaur homes. Look at them. Some are all jagged and pointed, and the tops of some look like they'd been sliced off with a knife. I wouldn't be at all surprised to see a dinosaur come crawling out of one of those cracks."

"You'd be more likely to see a rattlesnake," snorted Joey. "Dinosaurs have been dead millions of years. The professor said so."

"I know. But as long as they left their bones, and we get paid for them, it doesn't matter."

The professor was so absorbed in his work that he didn't see them until Daisy Belle came up to the beginning of the ravine on which he was working. When they called to him, he looked up, startled, then an expression of embarrassment crept across his face.

"I didn't do it again, did I?" he asked sheepishly.

They nodded, grinning, and he carefully climbed down to them.

Professor Harris was a small man and exceedingly thin. His hair was light, and under his broad-brimmed hat his face was burned scarlet from the sun. It never seemed to tan, but burned and peeled, and the new skin burned all over again. It must have been painful, but he never mentioned it. He wore rather thick-lensed glasses, a long-sleeved plaid shirt, and high boots which laced nearly up to his knees. The boots were a protection against rattlesnakes which often sunned themselves on rocky ledges. From the back pocket of the professor's trousers protruded the handles of several chisels and the brush of a whisk broom, which might be needed to brush away sedimentary flakes and sand if he found what he was seeking and had to chip the fossil from a rock.

"Have you found anything?" demanded Joan eagerly.

"Not yet." The professor shook his head regretfully. "But remember, I've only just started."

"It's been three weeks," Joey reminded him.

"Only a start," insisted the professor. "Many scientists have been at it for years with no more results than I."

Joey scowled. It seemed to him a very slow way to make money.

"What makes you think any may be here at all?" asked Joan, sitting down in the small shade of a clump of sagebrush and holding out the lunch bucket.

"The conditions are right," said the professor thoughtfully. "This is sedimentary rock. The surface is cut into ravines and gullies and canyons. This is dry country. There's no vegetation to protect the soil from wind and weather. It's true that I have found no bits of bone to lead me into my search, but there are discolorations in the rocks themselves. And if I keep looking, I hope to find the existence of bones."

"I should think an animal of some kind, a coyote maybe, would carry the bones away and chew on them," said Joan.

"Not these bones," Joey reminded her superiorly. "They're turned to stone, aren't they, Professor?"

"That's right," the professor agreed, biting into a thick sandwich. "A fossil is made when the action of water dripping through removes the animal matter and replaces it with mineral. No coyote would tackle a fossil, Joan. It would break his teeth."

"It must take a long time to do that," she said thoughtfully.

"The last dinosaur lived sixty million years ago," agreed the professor.

The twins remained while the professor ate his sandwiches, and as soon as he went back to hunting fossils they started home. It was now a little past noon, and the sun was almost directly overhead. It beat down on them unmercifully. Their cotton shirts clung damply against their skin, and little rivulets ran down their faces.

"I sure see why cowboys wear hats," said Joey grimly.

"Me too. We ought to make one for Daisy Belle if we're going to bring her out into the sun."

Today Daisy Belle seemed to suffer from the heat even more than they. Her head drooped, and she seemed scarcely able to lift one foot after another.

"Let's walk awhile," suggested Joey. "It's mean to make her carry us when we've got legs."

"All right," agreed Joan. "Only I don't know how far I can walk without sitting down to rest. The sun seems to make spots in my eyes, and when I look out there at those heat waves dancing across the ground I get dizzy."

"Don't look at them then," advised Joey. "Look at the cliffs instead. It's better that way."

"How can I look at the cliffs when they're going to be behind me?"

"They don't have to be," pointed out Joey. "Not right away, anyway. We can walk along the side of them instead of cutting across to the road the way we came."

"We'll have to cut across sometime," Joan reminded him, but she followed along without further argument.

Joey walked ahead, leading Daisy Belle. He kept as close to the edge of the rimrock cliffs as he could, holding a westward course which ran parallel with the road almost a mile to his left. He kept his eyes on the ground, shaking his head from time to time to rid himself of a fresh trickle of perspiration running down his face. It was too much effort to take out a handkerchief and wipe it off.

He was not sure afterward how it happened, but suddenly he felt the leather strap with which he had been leading Daisy Belle jerk out of his hands. He sensed, rather than saw, her rear in alarm and give a whinny of fright. At the same moment he heard the brittle rattle from his right, and, even before he turned, he knew what it was. A rattlesnake! Exactly what had alarmed the reptile he could not be sure, but that dry warning meant only one thing. The rattlesnake was going to strike.

Both twins realized instinctively that they ought to get out of the way. They ought to race after Daisy Belle across the dusty plain. Neither could move. They stood, too frightened to stir, staring down at the rocky ledge beside them where the snake was coiled. Then, as they looked, the rattlesnake was gone, covered completely by something round and padded and big as a large dishpan.

Their eyes moved upward from the round cover, and they saw that it continued into a leg, a stout, short leg that was joined onto the body of the most curious and frightening animal they had ever seen. He was larger than the biggest elephant, but, unlike an elephant, he was not all gray. He seemed to be many colors, browns and tans, grays, and yellows which deepened in places into orange. He was, in fact, so nearly the color of the rimrock cliffs, and his shape was so jagged and irregular, that when he stood against the rocks he blended in such a way as to make him almost invisible. Along his backbone ran a double row of sharp-edged triangular horns, the largest of which were two feet high, and the long, ten-foot tail which trailed behind him bore four upright spikes made of horn, each of which was about three feet tall. Moreover, this tail was not stationary but moved constantly from side to side, so that one moment they had a glimpse of the formidable spikes from one side of his body, and the next moment they appeared from the other. His front legs, one of which still remained on the lifeless rattlesnake, were considerably shorter than the back ones. This gave him the appearance of being humped up behind, and brought his low-hung head closer to the children. It was really a very small head, with a mouth that slightly resembled a parrot's beak, and tiny, bright, unblinking eyes.

Joan moaned with fright, and the animal looked in her direction. The whole head turned with the eyes as it did so.

"You should say thank you," said the creature. His voice, like his head, seemed much too small for the body. It was just an ordinary voice, such as you would expect to hear in any human being, but there was no inflection of words. They all came out in the same tone.

"Thank you," answered Joan automatically. Then she remembered that animals, except parrots and magpies possibly, don't speak English, and her mouth fell open in even greater amazement.

"A-are you a dragon?" stammered Joey.

"No," said the creature without surprise. "I don't know

14

what that is. I am a stegosaurus."

"And I don't know what that is," admitted Joey boldly. "Stego — What was it you said now?"

"Steg-o-sau-rus," repeated the creature, pausing a long time between each syllable. Then after a moment, "I'm a dinosaur."

"But there aren't such things," denied Joey. "At least, not any more."

"So far as I know, I am the only one left," admitted the stegosaurus. "I assure you, it is a lonely life."

"Are you going to eat us?" quavered Joan. It was all very well to stand and hold polite conversation with this dreadful dinosaur, but she preferred not to be kept in suspense.

"What do you take me for?" demanded the stego- saurus sharply, and the giant tail stopped moving from left to right. "Tyrannosaurus? Or Allosaurus? Certainly not. I am a vegetarian. You do not appeal to me in that way at all. And, if you're going to be insulting, I shall just go away. I wondered at the time if it wasn't a mistake showing myself just to save your lives."

"Oh, please don't," cried Joey.

"I'm sorry," said Joan quickly. "I didn't mean to hurt your feelings."

"You must be very careful," said the stegosaurus. "I know I'm stupid. Everyone says so, so it must be true. But I am sensitive, and I do get my feelings hurt easily."

"I won't do it again," she promised.

Slowly the spiked tail began to move once more.

Gently at first, then faster until it was swinging back and forth like a clock pendulum. Why, he wags it like a dog, thought Joan. When he's pleased about something, his tail wags to show that he is.

"How come you can talk?" demanded Joey.

"Can't everything?"

"Oh, no. Only people."

"Perhaps I'm a people," said the stegosaurus slowly. He seemed to consider this, for the motions of the tail grew slower for a moment. "No," he decided finally. "I'm sure I'm a dinosaur and a stegosaurus. I suppose I must have been born knowing how to talk, since I'm too stupid to learn. Perhaps people are stupid too."

"Some of them are," agreed Joey.

"Good," said the stegosaurus, his tail flashing fast from side to side. "We have something in common. I'm so glad now that I did come to your rescue as I did. That was instinct, you know. No one taught me to do it. If I had thought about it, I probably wouldn't have. Then I wouldn't have had this nice chat with you two. You have no idea how lonely I've been all these years with no one to talk to. No friends at all. You see, I'm shy."

"We'll be your friends," promised Joan, anxious to make up for the careless remark which had hurt the reptile's feelings.

"Thank you. Thank you," accepted the stegosaurus. "Then you must call me by my first name, and I'll call you by yours."

"All right," agreed Joey promptly. "I'm Joey. And she's

Joan. What's your name?"

The stegosaurus stepped forward eagerly, then halted. The tail stopped, poised in mid-air, and the tiny head moved from side to side ponderously. After a long moment it turned from one child to another, the bright beady eyes staring as though in an appeal for help.

"I don't know," it admitted. "It has been so many million years since anyone called me by my name, I've forgotten what it is."

"That's too bad," sympathized Joey. "But when you think about it, it will probably come back to you."

"But that's just it. I can't depend on it. My brain is too small to be of any use. I'll never know my name again."

"Then why don't we give you a new one?" said Joan quickly. "Unless you'd rather be called Stegosaurus."

"Only for formal occasions," said the dinosaur quickly. "And not by my friends even then. Oh, please give me a new name. A pretty one."

"Our horse is named Daisy Belle," said Joan thoughtfully. "Of course, she's a lady."

"And you're a man, aren't you?" added Joey. When the stegosaurus nodded, he began reciting all the men's names he could think of. "John, Peter, Dick, Bob, Paul, Roger, Jim, Steve — "

"Something a wee bit longer," urged the stegosaurus. "With more depth."

"Horace, Percy, Clarence, Andrew," suggested Joan.

"Milton, Harold, Richard, Victor, George," interrupted Joey, when he himself was interrupted in turn.

18

"George!" decided the stegosaurus. "I like that. I like the sound of it against my teeth. Any time you want me, just call 'George.' I'll know that it's my two friends calling, and I'll come."

He stepped back against the face of the cliff. Although they were watching every moment, the colors blended so completely with the rocks it was as though he had vanished. They could not see which way he went.

Chapter Two

"Now, CHILDREN," said the professor earnestly, "what you think you saw is impossible. It just couldn't happen."

"But it did," insisted Joey.

"He stepped out from the rocks and killed the rattlesnake that was going to strike us," said Joan. "And then we talked awhile, and he told us he was a stegosaurus, but he'd forgotten his first name, so we helped him pick out a new one. It's George."

"It's this horrible sun," wailed Mrs. Brown. "They've had a sunstroke. I knew it the minute they came home with this wild story. I made them lie down in a darkened room, but they don't seem to get over it. I think I should call a doctor."

"They seem to be cool enough now," objected the professor, touching them each on the cheek. "As cool as I am, anyway. No, I think it's more likely to be a game that children play sometimes."

"A game?" quavered Mrs. Brown.

"It's no game," said Joey indignantly. "I tell you, we saw him. Just as plain as we see you. We talked to him."

"George is a very nice stegosaurus," insisted Joan. "He doesn't eat people. He's a vegetarian."

"Of course," said the professor indulgently. He turned to Mrs. Brown and spoke reassuringly. "Psychologists tell us this is a very common behavior in small children. Sometimes they are lonely, so they create imaginary companions. They talk to them, play with them, and believe in them so strongly that the imaginary playmates actually become real to them."

"But Joey and Joan aren't really small children," protested Mrs. Brown. "And they can't be too lonely. They have each other."

"A delayed reaction," soothed the professor. "Remember that until a few months ago they lived in town and had many children to play with. Now that there are only two of them, the contrast may create a feeling of aloneness."

"Then we'd better move back to town," declared Mrs. Brown. "No matter what you say, I don't think this is natural. I don't like it at all."

"No, Mom," cried Joey. "Please don't. Let us stay a little longer, anyway."

"We'll never talk about George any more," promised Joan. "We aren't lonesome. Really. And what would become of Daisy Belle?"

"It's really nothing to be alarmed about," said the professor. "It's just imagination. They have been exceedingly interested in dinosaurs. They've asked lots of questions, and I've done my best to answer them. Curiosity is a healthy sign in children. Education and advancement spring from native curiosity about the world."

"I suppose so," admitted Mrs. Brown reluctantly. "But it's very naughty of them to frighten me so. I was sure it was a sunstroke."

"Yes, it was naughty," agreed the professor, looking at the twins severely. "Truth and fancy are two separate things. They must be recognized as such. Now you children really know that there isn't such a thing as a living dinosaur, don't you?"

The twins regarded each other with understanding eyes. Since they were so very much alike, it was sometimes possible for them to reach an agreement without speaking aloud.

"Well, if there were, he would be awfully old," admitted Joey. "You wouldn't think anything could live that long."

"Certainly not." The professor nodded vigorously. "The last dinosaur lived sixty million years ago. Do you realize how long ago that was? The stegosaurus, with whom you claim a speaking acquaintance, lived even longer ago. He was from the Jurassic, or the second period, in the age of reptiles."

"Was he dumb?" asked Joan earnestly.

"Dumb? Oh, he might have been able to make sounds. He very probably did have a voice. But he certainly couldn't speak English."

"I didn't mean that," she corrected. "I mean was he dumb — stupid?"

"Oh, very stupid." The professor nodded emphatically. "The stegosaurus had a brain the size of a walnut. You couldn't have selected a more stupid dinosaur for your playmate if you had tried."

"How can you be sure he was stupid?" asked Joey stubbornly. "Just because his brain was small doesn't prove anything. It might have been different from ours. Maybe it didn't have to be very big. The inside of a watch is small, but just look how it runs!"

"It's hardly the same thing," smiled the professor. He looked at Mrs. Brown indulgently, then warmed to his subject. "The stegosaurus had a very unusual spinal column. There was an enlargement nearly twenty times the size of the brain on the creature's back. For a time people thought the stegosaurus had two brains because of this, but it wasn't so. It was the nerve center which controlled the movements of the heavy hind limbs and powerful tail."

"You mean so he could wag his tail like a dog?" asked Joan quickly.

"Oh, I hadn't thought of that," said the professor lightly. "But he could certainly move his tail. There were heavy spikes on it, you see; and if the stegosaurus were attacked by one of the meat-eating dinosaurs, he could whip his tail from side to side and rip open his attacker."

The twins looked at each other again and nodded thoughtfully.

"What made them all die?" asked Joey after a moment.

"A combination of several things. The physical changes of the country, perhaps. The mountain ranges weren't here at the time of the dinosaurs. The land was swampy, and the swamps dried up. The dinosaurs who ate swamp vegetation had no way of getting food, and with their poor brains they didn't know where to look for it. They died off, and that left the meat-eating dinosaurs without food. Warm-blooded animals appeared and ate the dinosaur eggs, so no new ones hatched. The next thing they were all gone."

"So now that you see how silly it sounds, let's hear no more about a talking dinosaur," said Mrs. Brown firmly. "Supper's been waiting a long time, Joey, please put the chairs around the table."

Realizing that a further discussion of dinosaurs would distress their mother, the twins spoke of other things during dinner. Mrs. Brown was having a difficult time adjusting herself to the change of climate and the disappointment of the ranch. It wouldn't take very much to convince her that they must go back to town immediately. The children did not want to leave Cricket Creek. They were not lonely, as the professor claimed. It was fun living in the country by themselves. There was Daisy Belle, on whom they could take rides. There was the tumbling old barn to play in, and it was a contest against the weather to coax the garden to grow. There were strange insects, and every once in a while they caught a glimpse of a jack rabbit, or at night, safe in their beds, they heard the distant call of a coyote. Besides, any day the professor might unearth a valuable fossil which would mean a lot of money and solve the family Problem.

They wisely decided to say no more about George in the hearing of adults, but every day they discussed him when they were alone.

"Maybe we did imagine him," worried Joan. "Maybe it was too much sun."

"Would we both imagine the same thing?" demanded Joey.

"I don't see why not. We're twins. We look alike, and lots of times we think alike. Besides, it was the same sun shining down on both of us."

"That has nothing to do with it," said Joey flatly. "We saw George. And we talked to him. You know it as well as I do."

"I guess so," agreed Joan hesitantly.

"The thing that makes me mad" — Joey frowned — "is that nobody believes us. We've made a discovery that ought to be worth a lot of money. If the professor will pay money just for the bones of an old dead dinosaur, just think how much he'd pay for a live one."

"But Joey! We couldn't do that. It wouldn't be right to sell George. Besides, he doesn't belong to us."

"Why not? He's on our land."

"That still doesn't make him ours."

"What would he do with the money himself?" snorted Joey in disgust. "He'd probably be very glad to let us have it. Look. If we told people about our discovery, we'd be famous. And so would he. He could live in a nice zoo somewhere, and they'd bring him his dinner every day, and people would come and talk to him so he'd never be lonesome any more."

"I guess that's right," admitted Joan doubtfully.

"Why, George would never have to work again as long as he lived."

"I don't think he works now."

"Well, hunt for food then. Or find some place to get out of the rain and snow. Everything would be done for him."

"Maybe."

"The thing we'll have to do is convince him of that. We'll have to show him how nice things would be."

"But how will we find a zoo that wants him?"

"We'll let the professor take care of that. If he knows somebody who wants bones, he'll know somebody who wants a live stegosaurus. We'll just get George to come home with us and introduce him to the professor, and that's all there is to it."

"I can just see his face," grinned Joan. "The professor's, I mean, when George comes walking in."

"Me too." Joey nodded. "Now if the professor would just forget his lunch again, or Mom would let us go for a ride, we'd find George and everything would be fixed."

But the professor was careful to take his lunch with him when he left every morning. And Mrs. Brown, who still insisted that the sun had something to do with the strange behavior of her two children, refused to let them venture away from the ranch. A week went by, and the twins fussed and worried and rehearsed the speech they would make to George which would convince him that life in a zoo was preferable to one in the unprotected open.

One morning they awoke and there were white clouds piled like meringue on the horizon. It was hotter than ever, and the air was still and motionless. There must have been wind higher up, however, for the line of meringue kept growing larger and moving nearer.

"Thunderclaps," said Mrs. Brown. "A good storm is just what we need to clear the atmosphere."

The storm reached Cricket Creek by midmorning. The whole sky was overcast by this time, and thunder cracked overhead and echoed in great deafening booms against the slopes. It rained after each clap with such violence that the poor garden vegetables were crushed to the ground, and Cricket Creek filled and ran with saffron water instead of mud. Mrs. Brown opened all the doors and windows to let in fresh, cooling air.

"Ordinarily I don't like thunder," she told the twins. "But this is one storm I'm glad to see."

"I wonder if George got out of the rain," whispered Joan.

"Sh!" warned Joey, glaring at his sister.

The storm cleared the atmosphere as Mrs. Brown had hoped it would, and, once the rain stopped, she agreed that the twins might go for a ride. Joey put the blanket on Daisy Belle with fingers that trembled with eagerness.

"This time tomorrow we'll be famous," he assured Joan. "Rich, and very, very famous. We can buy a whole herd of horses, and some cows, and hire cowboys to take care of them until I learn how to do it myself. And Mom will never have to work out again, and we'll have a car like the professor's, only new, and a television set."

"And I'll have a pink bedroom," added Joan. "With a dressing table with a ruffled skirt, and a pink bedspread, and pink rugs on the floor."

"Ha!" snorted Joey. "I'll sleep in the new bunkhouse with the cowboys."

They crossed the slightly steaming plain to the rocks where they had met the stegosaurus a week ago and dismounted.

"You'd better hobble Daisy Belle a little way off," warned Joan. "We don't want her to run away again. It was a long walk home."

"What do you think I'm doing?" asked Joey in a superior tone.

Daisy Belle was securely tied to a large jagged rock a short distance away so she would not be startled by the

appearance of the stegosaurus. Then the twins walked back toward the spot where they had first encountered the reptile.

"George!" called Joey loudly. "Oh, George!"

They waited expectantly, but no multicolored dinosaur appeared from behind one of the jutting crags.

"George!" called Joan in her sweetest tones. "Oh, George. It's us. Your friends. Remember? It's Joey and Joan come to see you."

They waited again, then both of them began calling at once, running this way and that, peering behind rocks, making cups of their hands so that the sound would carry farther. There was no answer to their call, no sign of an armored dinosaur with wagging spiked tail.

"Maybe he's gone away," said Joan.

"I don't think so," objected Joey. "He would have told us if he'd planned to do anything like that. Don't you remember? He said to call and he'd come."

"He may have forgotten. Or maybe"—Joan's eyes grew round with disappointment — "maybe he wasn't here at all. Maybe the professor's right. And Mom. Maybe we just imagined him."

"Phooey!" said Joey loudly. But he looked a little uneasy at the idea. "We've just got to call louder, that's all."

They kept calling for the better part of an hour before even Joey agreed that it was useless. If the stegosaurus heard them, he refused to be coaxed out of hiding. Perhaps he had decided he didn't want to be friends. Or perhaps they had been mistaken. Perhaps there wasn't a stegosaurus after all.

"Well, come on," said Joey dejectedly. "We might as well go home."

Joan followed him back down the rocks, stepping carefully lest some of the loosened sediment give way under her feet. Suddenly she came up against her brother with a resounding thump. Joey had stopped still in his tracks.

"There!" he cried excitedly. "That proves it!"

"What does?" asked Joan, trying to peer over his shoulder.

He moved out of the way to let her see, his finger pointing to the lowest ledge of rock near the road. Atop the ledge was the completely flattened body of a rattlesnake.

"We didn't imagine it," said Joey in a pleased tone. "He was here all right. Nothing could smash a big rattler like that except a dinosaur's foot."

Chapter Three

BEFORE THE ARRIVAL of Professor Harris, groceries had been a problem at the ranch on Cricket Creek. The Browns had brought a sizable stock with them in the moving van, but they had expected to grow much of their own food supply. When they realized that was impossible, trips to the nearest village, some fifteen miles away, became a necessity. Their only means of transportation was old Daisy Belle, but there was no saddle for her and no wagon for her to pull. They had been dependent upon the generosity of a neighbor, Mr. Blackwood, who always stopped by on his own trips into Silo to see if they needed anything.

When Professor Harris arrived and realized the situation, he insisted on driving Mrs. Brown into town once a week.

"It won't take more than an hour," he declared. "What's an hour, more or less, when I may be at this every summer for several years?"

They departed for one of these shopping expeditions on a morning a few days after the thunderstorm, leaving

Joey and Joan to water the garden. It had to be done before the sun was well up, and they usually repeated the proceedings after sunset. The thirsty earth drank water like a sponge.

"The carrots have come back pretty good," remarked Joan. "Their leaves were all smashed in the mud after that rain, but it doesn't seem to have hurt them much."

"You can't hurt a carrot," said Joey. "Anyway, the part you eat is all underground. But I don't think we'll ever have any corn."

"Good morning, my friends," said a flat, monotonous voice behind them.

They whirled around, startled, to see the stegosaurus regarding them with bright, expressionless eyes. Against the flat, brown backdrop of the hill his colors stood out distinctly, and his spiked tail wagged back and forth like a study in perpetual motion.

"George!" cried Joan in delight and surprise. It was amazing that so large a creature could move about without making a great amount of noise. Then she realized that each of the massive feet was padded with a thick, cushionlike substance.

"Where have you been?" demanded Joey reproachfully. "We came to see you and called and called."

"I did not hear you," explained George. "I must have been asleep. When the rain began, I thought cold weather had set in, so I went to my cave. It was not a sound sleep, however, nor a long one. It lasted only a few days. Then I woke up."

"We nearly screamed our heads off," said Joey. "It must have been sounder than you thought."

"I am sorry," apologized George. "When I woke up, I seemed to need something. It wasn't food. I tried that. It wasn't sleep. Instinct told me there was only one thing left, companionship. So I came looking for you. I took a great chance coming here. I hope we won't be disturbed."

"There's no one else around. And we're glad you came, George," said Joey heartily. "Because we've got a plan."

"A plan?" said George. "What is a plan?"

"A plan is when you figure out something to do. And then you do it."

"I have never made a plan," confessed George. "I couldn't, you see. It must take large brains to make a plan, and mine is too small. I act on instinct."

"You don't have to make one," Joey assured him. "We made it for you. It's a plan so that you'll never be lonely again. And you'll never have to hunt for food —"

"But I don't have to hunt for food," objected George. "It's all around me."

"What do you eat?"

"Sagebrush. It's very tasty. Especially after a rain. Try some." George turned his head, and the beaklike mouth fluttered as he nibbled at the nearest clump of sagebrush.

"Well, but —" Joey hesitated, then went on firmly.

"And you wouldn't have to sleep in a cold old cave. You could have a nice warm cage with straw in it."

"Cage?" interrupted George. "What is a cage?"

"Well, it's like a little room, only it doesn't have walls. It has bars."

"Why?" asked George.

Joey was suddenly ashamed. Joan had been right. George wouldn't like to be shut in. But the stegosaurus was regarding him intently, and he had to go on.

"So no one can get inside with you."

"No one tries to share my cave with me," said George firmly. "Although I am a sound sleeper, I do thresh around. Warm-blooded animals, as well as other dinosaurs, stay far away from my tail. I see no reason for the bars. They would be no protection from the wind and cold."

"Oh, the cage would be inside. It would be warm."

"What do you mean — inside? Inside of what?"

"Oh, like in a house."

"What is a house?"

"That's a house," said Joan, pointing. "We live in it."

"Then it's your cave," decided George. "I have one already, thank you. Quite comfortable. Now please go on about this plan you mentioned."

"Well, it's a plan so you'd never be lonesome," said Joey desperately. "People would come to see you. Lots of people. They'd come all the time and look at you and talk to you."

The giant tail stopped wagging, and the stegosaurus

seemed to waver on his sturdy feet.

"Oh no, no!" he objected. His voice, while still a monotone, rose a note in alarm. "You don't understand. I shouldn't like that at all. I told you. I'm shy. I can't stand to meet strangers."

"But you met us."

"That was an accident," said George. "I told you how it happened. My instinct was to save you, so I did. Once we had met, my instinct was to stay and chat. I did, and we became friends. But you must not ask me to meet any other strangers."

"But George," began Joey.

"Promise me," insisted the stegosaurus. "Promise you will keep our friendship a secret. I should die if I had to meet another stranger. I really would, and the world would be without a single, solitary dinosaur."

"Of course we promise," said Joan quickly.

"I think you'd like them once you met them," insisted Joey. "Especially the professor. He loves dino- saurs. He's digging for dinosaur bones every day."

"The ghoul!" cried George. "Disturbing the burial grounds of my people! I never heard of anything so dis- gusting. Never! How would you like it if somebody went around digging up the bones of your relatives?"

"I wouldn't," agreed Joan promptly.

"This is different," said Joey. "They aren't bones any more. They've turned to stone."

"Perhaps it's my small brain which keeps me from seeing the difference, but I can't at all," said George. He moved closer to the clump of sagebrush and began to eat rapidly. The bush seemed to disappear before their very eyes.

"You'll have to excuse me for talking with my mouth full," he apologized. "But whenever I get upset or nervous it gives me the most tremendous appetite. If I get exceedingly upset, I sharpen my tail. But that's only when things are very bad."

"Now see what you've done," whispered Joan indignantly. "I told you it wouldn't work. He wouldn't like it at all, and George is our friend. He's eating so fast he'll probably get indigestion. And that will be your fault too."

"I never really thought of it that way, George," admitted Joey. "I was just trying to keep you from being lonesome. Besides, I thought we could make a little money, and we do need that."

"Money? What is money?" demanded George.

"Why, it's either paper or metal. And you give it to somebody, and they give you something for it."

"It's my small brain," apologized the stegosaurus. "I just can't understand that at all."

"It's sort of like this," explained Joan, trying to find a medium of exchange which George could appreciate. Food, shelter, clothing, all the things one ordinarily buys with money, had to be eliminated in his case. "You gave us your friendship, and we gave you ours. You see, we each gave the other something. It's an exchange."

"Of course." George nodded, his beady eyes glistening.

"I saved your lives, and you won't tell any strangers who might come around about me. That's our exchange. It's fair, isn't it?"

"Yes," agreed Joey after a minute. "That's fair. I promise."

"You know," said George, after a moment during which he continued to chew rapidly, "the sagebrush down here by your cave has a slightly different flavor from that growing beside mine." He jerked out the remainder of the bush by the roots, gulped it down, and moved on to another. "It makes a nice change."

"Wouldn't you like to try a carrot?" suggested Joan hospitably, pulling one up.

George advanced and took it from her hand. Slowly at first, then rapidly, it disappeared into the beaklike mouth, finishing off with the fringed green leaves on the end.

"Thank you," he said. "A little flat, but edible, as almost everything is if you can just learn to like it, and I can. That's always been one of my faults, or virtues, if you want to look at it that way. I've known dinosaurs who would eat only water plants. If they couldn't get water plants, they starved. Other dinosaurs starved when they couldn't get meat, but I see no reason to be so proud. So long as I can chew it, I'll eat it. I differ from the others in my family in this regard."

"Would you eat meat if you couldn't get plants?" demanded Joan suspiciously. "The last time we met you said you were a vegetarian."

"I should hate to come to that," admitted George.

"And I doubt if I ever have to. Lately there always seems to be a good crop of sagebrush. Sagebrush and water—that's enough for any stegosaurus. At least it's enough for me."

"Water!" cried Joey. "Where do you get the water?"

"Why, from the hidden river of course," answered George carelessly. Suddenly his tail stopped in mid-air. "Strangers are coming!" he said. "My instinct tells me it's time to go."

Before they could open their mouths to say good-by, he turned and went lumbering up the slope. For a creature his size, the stegosaurus made remarkably good progress, and in a few moments he had reached the top and disappeared.

"Joan! Did you hear him? Do you know what he said?" cried Joey, turning to his sister in excitement. "He knows about a hidden river! It can't be too far from those cliffs where he lives."

"I suppose so," she agreed. "Everything has to have water sometimes. Even camels. Probably even dinosaurs."

"But if it's on our land, it's going to mean a fortune. We can irrigate with it! We can grow things! We can make money!"

"You and your fortunes," said Joan impatiently. "You were going to make a fortune selling George to a zoo, remember?"

"I have to think of such things. I'm the man of the family," said Joey with dignity. "Besides, this is different.

This is a hidden river in a country where there just isn't any water. Oh, wait till I tell Mom. Wait till I tell the professor!"

"What'll you tell them?" demanded Joan. "That our stegosaurus was here? That we talked to him again? And that he told us he got his drinking water from a hidden river?"

"No, I guess I can't at that," admitted Joey. "We promised George we wouldn't admit we knew him. And if we should let it slip, Mom will think we've had another sunstroke and make us go back to town."

"So you'll just have to forget it."

"I can't forget it. Don't you realize we're the only ranch around here that doesn't have water of some kind besides what we get from the well?" He glared up at the sun which was beginning to gather strength for the day. "We'll just have to get George to show it to us and then pretend we found it ourselves."

"He's likely to want us to bring other people around where it is, isn't he?" she scoffed. "Can't you get it through your head? He's shy. He doesn't want anyone around but us. It's *his* hidden river, and I bet he wants it to stay hidden."

"Nuts," said Joey. He kicked at a clod of dirt, and it rolled over to land in one of the holes left by George when he had torn out the sagebrush bushes. There were a dozen or more of them, and they left a cleared circle in the dry ground.

"Here they come," announced Joan. "George has good

ears, even if he does have instinct instead of a brain."

The professor's old car appeared at the road atop the slope, gathered speed as it came down, and stopped with a loud squealing of brakes. The twins walked over to help carry groceries.

"It's getting hot already," Mrs. Brown complained. "Did you finish watering the garden?"

"They did more than that," exclaimed the professor in surprise, staring at the cleared space where George had been standing. "They've started to clear out sagebrush to make an even larger garden next year."

"Why, so they have," agreed Mrs. Brown. "They've even carried the roots and branches away too."

The twins looked at each other significantly but said nothing. They dutifully carried in an armload of groceries, but when they came back for more, Joey turned to his sister.

"You know," he said, "I think we've discovered what stegosaurus are good for. There must be hundreds of people who want to have land cleared off, and he'll eat anything. If we could just line up the jobs for George, we could make a fortune. He could work at night, and no one would see him."

"Oh, be quiet," said Joan crossly. "You make me sick."

Chapter Four

Friends are supposed to help each other," insisted Joey, turning his head to speak over his shoulder.

"Sure, they are," agreed Joan. "But they aren't supposed to hurt themselves doing it. And if you ask somebody to do something for you, and he hurts himself doing it, then you aren't being a good friend."

The twins, astride old Daisy Belle, were on their way to the cliffs. Ever since Joey had conceived his new ideas on making money, he had been so excited he could hardly restrain himself. Since both ideas — a hidden river to supply water for the ranch and an easy way to clear the land of sagebrush — depended on George, it was necessary to consult the stegosaurus before continuing further.

"I'm not doing anything to hurt him," he maintained. "Didn't I give up the idea of a zoo right away when I saw he wouldn't like it? But I don't see why he needs a whole river for himself. He could certainly let us have a little of it. And as for clearing off sagebrush, I told you he could work at night when nobody could see him. Besides, eating isn't work. Everybody has to eat."

"Well, you can ask him, I guess," agreed Joan reluctantly. "But if he says no, don't you tease."

"You just don't understand these things. I suppose it's because you're a girl," said Joey in a superior tone. "But I'm the man of the family, and I know we have to make some money. I'm just trying to figure out a way to do it."

Joan shut her lips tightly to keep back the angry retort. Usually she understood her twin better than anyone else, but there were times when she wanted to spank him.

At the cliffs Joey tied Daisy Belle at a safe distance. Then they walked back to the spot where they had first met their new friend and called. This time there was an almost immediate answer. The stegosaurus came padding silently down the cliff on sure but cumbersome feet. As before, he seemed to evolve out of the rocks, and if it hadn't been for the wagging tail, they might have had to look twice to see him.

"My little friends," greeted George, turning his head to inspect them each in turn. "How nice to see you again so soon. I only just left you."

"You only just left us?" cried Joan in surprise.

"Why, yes. Don't you remember? I came to call on you at your cave."

"But that was three days ago," objected Joey.

"Time is nothing to me," explained George. "A day and an hour are all the same. Even one year is nothing,

44

when you've lived as long as I have."

"How do you count time?" demanded Joan.

"By sleeps," said George promptly. "I sleep whenever the weather is cold and as long as it remains that way. I wake up when it's warm. Of course, I don't pretend to keep track of how many times I sleep or how often I wake. My brain is too small to learn counting. But come, come. I'm forgetting my manners. You've come to call, and I must entertain you properly. Would you care for a little sagebrush?"

"No, thank you," said Joan. "We had breakfast before we left home."

"But I would like a drink of water. I'm thirsty," added Joey quickly.

"Of course," agreed George. "We'll go to the hidden river at once. You may have all the water you wish. There seems to be an inexhaustible supply."

The stegosaurus started briskly up the cliffs, and the children followed, keeping a safe distance to avoid the wagging tail. Joan's face was troubled, but Joey's was eager and excited.

"Does anyone but you know about this river, George?" he asked.

"No, I don't think so." George turned his head to speak over his shoulder. He had to turn his whole body to do so, for the great horns along his backbone rose high in the air. They were not attached in pairs, but each row was set diagonally to the other. "There was a man with a skin not pale like yours, but reddish in color, who found

46

the river once. That was several sleeps ago. I watched him from the rocks, but he did not see me."

"An Indian," said Joey quickly.

"He did not stay," continued George, as though he had not heard. "He came upon the river suddenly. Then he turned and hurried away. He did not come back, and he must have told no one about it, because no one came after that. I was glad, of course."

"Why were you glad?" demanded Joan.

"Because I am shy," explained George patiently. "I do not want to share my river with strangers. I would not want to go there and be discovered."

"I told you so," Joan said to Joey triumphantly.

"But George, that's sort of selfish," said Joey, ignoring his sister. "There's not much water in this part of the country. If there's a river, it ought to be shared by everybody."

The stegosaurus stopped still, and the spiked tail drooped with dejection.

"I never thought of that," he admitted after a moment. "You're right, of course. A river is for everyone. It wasn't put here just for me."

"Maybe it was," argued Joan. "If you hadn't had the water, you couldn't have stayed alive, could you?"

"I'm afraid not," said George. "But Joey's right. I've been very selfish. I thought only of myself and how lucky I was to have the water. It's such good water."

"Maybe we can figure out something," said Joey, touched by the stegosaurus' distress. "Maybe we could show the people where it runs, and they could take the water from farther downstream. Then you wouldn't be bothered at all."

"Oh, we couldn't do that," objected George. "That wouldn't work at all."

"Of course not," said Joan. "They'd trace it to its beginning and maybe build dams or things. In a country like this they'd have to if they wanted to irrigate."

"Well, come along," said George. "I'll show you my river, and you can do whatever your brains tell you must be done. The last thing in the world I want to be is selfish."

They climbed up cliffs and scrambled down ledges. The dinosaur moved effortlessly, steadying himself with the end of his tail whenever the crumbling sediment seemed about to give way beneath him. But the twins, who had only two legs instead of four and had to grasp nearby rocks with their hands, did not fare so well. They were panting and breathless when George finally came to a halt.

"There it is!" he announced.

They had at last descended, and now they were in a gully encircled by jagged cliffs. Although they rubbed their eyes, there was no sign of a river. Instead, a thin cloud of steam seemed to rise from a place on the ground before them. All about it the rough ground seemed to be broken up in great clods, as though someone had been using a pickax. But they heard water. To their ears came a bubbling sound not too unlike the noise made by a teakettle just before it is ready to boil.

"Where's the river?" demanded Joey.

"There," answered George, pointing to the steaming place in the ground. "Drink all you like."

The twins advanced cautiously. Their noses were now filled with the sharp, biting tang of minerals. When they came close they could see the water. It bubbled a little as it came from the ground, and gave off the thin cloud of steam which they had seen from a distance.

"This isn't a river," cried Joey. "This is a hot spring!"

"The river is hidden. I told you that," said George. "It is hidden underground. But there must be a hidden river, or the water wouldn't escape at this point. It's probably like a waterfall, only in this case the water falls up instead of down."

"Don't try to explain it to him," whispered Joan. "You know he couldn't figure it out, and you might hurt his feelings."

"Men couldn't use this river," said Joey, choking down his disappointment. "It just wouldn't be any use to them."

"You mean I haven't been selfish after all?" cried George quickly. "Oh, that makes me feel much better. You have no idea how relieved I am."

"You haven't been one bit selfish," Joan told him. "And even if it had been a real river, the kind that runs on top of the earth, you wouldn't have been, either. Because it wouldn't have been your fault that people hadn't found it."

"Splendid!" exclaimed George. "What would I do without my friends? What did I do before I met you? You're such a comfort to me. You can't imagine. Come, let's all have a drink on that."

The stegosaurus advanced to the edge of the pool and, lowering his head, drank noisily of the scalding water. After a time he looked up.

"You're not drinking. I thought you were thirsty."

"I haven't a cup," explained Joey.

"What is a cup?"

"It's something to drink out of."

"Can't you drink without one?"

"I don't know," admitted Joey. He dipped a tentative finger in the hot spring and jerked it back quickly. "Ow!"

"What's the matter?" asked George.

"It burned me."

"I really don't know what you mean," said George, lowering his head to drink again.

Joan sat down on the dry ground and wiped the perspiration from her face. This little gully, protected by its rock walls and heated even further by the steam from the spring, left her almost without breath.

"Well, so much for your scheme to get rich quick," she told her brother.

"It never hurts to try," Joey answered indignantly. "If you don't try, you never get anywhere."

George left the spring and came over to join them. He didn't sit down, and Joan wondered if he could.

Obviously he must lie down to rest, for he had spoken of his long sleeps. Getting up and down must have been a problem for anyone so large and unwieldy, she decided, and wished he would try it now so that she could see how it was done.

"Now what can I do to entertain you?" asked George.

"Let's just talk," said Joey.

"I'd love to," agreed the stegosaurus. "Have you a special topic, or do we just stumble into one?"

"I'd like to talk about your food," said Joey firmly. "About sagebrush."

"A delicious subject," said George. "And the best thing about it is that it seems to go on and on. There's no end to it."

"Do you have special places where you like to get it?" persisted Joey. "Or do you just eat it where you happen to find it? What I mean is, is there a difference in sagebrush? You said the stuff that grows around our house had a little different taste."

"Yes, I believe it did," agreed George after a thoughtful pause. "But after all, it's much the same. Sometimes there seems a little greenness about it. That's when I first wake up from one of my sleeps. And after I've been up awhile, it gets a bit drier, but I'm really not particular. That's why I stay alive."

"Do you eat at night as well as in the daytime?"

"Night?"

"That's when it's dark and the sun goes down. It's when we sleep."

"Foolish of you," chided George. "It's one of the pleasantest times there is. You should learn to sleep only in cold weather as I do. Certainly I eat at night. In fact, that's when I do the most eating. There are fewer people around then, only an occasional coyote or a jack rabbit. I don't have to be afraid of being seen when the sun goes down."

"Well, would you mind eating sagebrush at a particular spot I told you about?" Joey steadily avoided Joan's glares of disapproval. "Would you mind very much doing that?"

"Certainly not," said George. "However, I think it's a very queer request. I probably won't be able to understand, but would you try to explain?"

"Sure I will. You see, people don't like sagebrush."

"Why not?"

"Because it's not good for anything."

"It's good for dinosaurs," insisted George. "If we were here in our former numbers, there wouldn't be enough to go around."

"It's lucky for you then that you're all alone," pointed out Joan.

"Why, so it is." George was pleased with the idea, and his tail wagged faster than ever. "Although, you must admit, it's a selfish thought."

"Anyway," continued Joey, determined not to be side-tracked, "men want to get rid of the sagebrush. If you ate in a particular spot every night, it wouldn't take too long for you to clear it all away."

"No," agreed George. "I've noticed that it doesn't grow back as quickly as I can eat it up."

"Then you'll do it?"

"Of course, dear friend. It will be my pleasure."

This time it was Joey's turn to look at his sister in triumph. Joan stood up.

"I think we'd better go," she said. "If we're gone too long, Mom will begin to worry."

George followed close at their heels as they started the steep climb out of the gully.

"Come again," he urged. "Come soon. And next time remember to bring a cup. I want you to share the delicious water from my hidden river."

Chapter Five

THE NEXT MORNING when they awoke, great clumps of sagebrush were missing from the yard. Ordinarily sagebrush scattered itself here and there over dry, arid land, but there was one place next to the old corral where it had spread to make a solid row. The row was completely wiped out.

"Look!" exclaimed Joey, when he and Joan came out to water the garden. "George was here last night."

"I hope he had a good dinner," said Joan.

It was an unusually hot day, and Mrs. Brown, who remained indoors, did not notice the absence of the sagebrush row, but the professor did.

He came back to the ranch house in the middle of the afternoon, such an unheard-of proceeding that the twins raced out to meet him. They had been playing in the shade of the old barn, attempting to stir field mice out of the stack of hay laid in for Daisy Belle's winter feeding.

"Is anything wrong?" called Joan anxiously. "Are you sick?"

"Did you find something?" cried Joey. "A dinosaur bone?"

The professor shook his head wearily. His red, peeling face looked more painful than ever today.

"It's very commendable of you to clear out the sagebrush," he said cautiously. "But it's a pretty hot day to be working. And besides, that row against the corral wasn't hurting anything. You'd hardly expect to plant anything there."

"It might seed itself," said Joey quickly. "It's better to clear it all out."

The professor smiled faintly and preceded them into the house.

"Are you sick?" asked Mrs. Brown in turn as they entered the kitchen. "Did you have too much of that terrible sun?"

"No," said the professor, finding himself a chair. "It isn't that. I just got to thinking."

"About what?" demanded Joey.

"I've been working this portion of the rocks for several weeks," said the professor slowly, "and so far I haven't found anything to substantiate my theory. Not a fragment or an indication of a bone. Not even an impression. I'm wondering if I shouldn't move farther on."

"You mean off our land?" said Joan anxiously.

"I'm afraid so."

"But you said yourself that people like you have to look and look before they find anything," protested Joey. "You said you'd only just started."

"That's true," admitted the professor. "But perhaps I've started in the wrong place."

"I just know dinosaurs were here once," insisted Joan, and bit her lip nervously.

"It's quite likely they were. In fact, I'm sure of it," agreed the professor. "But, unless you get some little clue as to where to start hunting, there's no use going on. I was misled by the discoloration in the rocks. I haven't found a bone or an impression."

"What's an impression?" demanded Joey shrewdly.

"It's a footprint," explained Professor Harris. "A dinosaur's footprint left in the rock."

"Do you think they could leave footprints in rock?" asked Joan doubtfully. "I know they were big and heavy, but maybe they weren't that heavy."

"The rocks weren't rocks then," explained the professor. "Places where impressions have been found were often parts of old river beds. They were soft at that time, and the dinosaur's feet sank and left deep imprints. The water level fell, and the mud dried up and baked in the sun. When the water rose again, sediment filled the tracks and made casts. After many, many years — thousands probably — the casts turned to stone."

"I've never seen anything like that around here," said Joey thoughtfully. "In the first place, there isn't any water."

"Don't forget this was all covered with water once," the professor reminded him. "These western states of ours were rolling swamps and part of the sea. There weren't any mountains."

"That's right," Joey nodded. "You told us, but I forgot."

"Professor Harris," pleaded Joan earnestly. "Don't give up yet. Please try just a little longer."

"Now, Joan," reproved Mrs. Brown. "The professor knows about this business and you don't. You mustn't ask him to waste his time looking for bones where there aren't any."

"But the footprints," insisted Joan. "That's different. We didn't know about them before."

"There's no reason why you should," said Mrs. Brown. "Professor Harris knew, and he's been watching for them."

"But I think — I just sort of remember seeing one of those once," stammered Joan. "Only, of course, I didn't know what it was."

"Where, Joan?" demanded the professor eagerly. "Where did you see something like that? What did it look like?"

"I don't know. I just can't remember. Only it seems to me that I did. Maybe it will come to me."

"I'm afraid her imagination's running away with her," apologized Mrs. Brown.

"It could be," admitted the professor. He wanted to believe that Joan had really seen something in the rocks which would turn out to be the impression of a dinosaur's foot.

"Couldn't you just stay a few days longer?" pleaded

Joan. She looked at Joey, her eyes asking for help. But this was one of the times Joey refused to cooperate or try to read her mind. He sat glumly, his face a scowl of disappointment. "Couldn't you just stay till the end of the week? I have a hunch that by then we'll find something."

"Well," smiled the professor, "if it means so much to you, and if you'll try very hard to remember where you saw those prints — "

"Thank you," she said gratefully. "I'll try. I'll try very hard. Come on, Joey." She tugged at her brother's arm until he got unwillingly to his feet. "Let's go back and find mice."

"Stay out of the sun," called Mrs. Brown after them.

"Of all the rotten luck," growled Joey, once they were alone. "Of course, it could be worse. I can line up the sagebrush-clearing jobs for George myself, but I've got sort of used to the professor. I like to have him around. And his board money helps until we get really going on my plan."

"You and your plan!" scoffed Joan. "So long as there's no water for crops, who's going to pay to have sagebrush cleared out? Joey, look. We just can't let the professor go. Not until his college opens next fall and he has to."

"It will be tough," agreed Joey. "His car sure helps about groceries. We'd be back to the neighbors again without it. Unless Mom would let me buy a saddle for Daisy Belle."

"You know she won't. Or ride into Silo alone if you had one. No, we've got to keep that board money coming in, and there's only one way to do it."

"How?"

"Find a dinosaur footprint for the professor."

"Oh, simple. Very, very simple. Boy, you sure are smart. If he can't find one himself, how can we?"

"We can't." Joan tried to keep her patience. "But George can."

"How do you know he can?"

"I mean I hope he can. He's lived here a long time. He's been all over those rocks. If there's a footprint there, he ought to know where it is."

"But would he tell us? You know what he said about the professor digging for dinosaur bones."

"This is different. He shouldn't care about a footprint. In fact, he should be very proud that people think a place where his ancestors once walked was so important."

"Maybe he would at that," agreed Joey, brightening. "And I expect the professor would pay us for a footprint just as quick as he'd pay for a bone."

"I'm sure he would," agreed Joan.

"Now the thing we've got to do," decided Joey, assuming command, "is to find George."

"That's the problem." Joan frowned. "Mom will never let us go riding today, as hot as it is. And tomorrow may be even hotter."

"Then we'll just have to wait till George comes to us."

"But that may not be for a long time. And the professor said he'd stay only till the end of the week."

"He'll come tonight," said Joey positively. "And you have me to thank for it too. He'll come to eat the rest of our sagebrush."

It seemed to the children that the remainder of the afternoon would never pass, but eventually it did. It was still daylight when they ate dinner, but as shadows began to creep out from the sides of the buildings, a tiny breeze sprang up. Mrs. Brown opened the doors and windows then, and they all sat on the back porch watching the western sky that flamed scarlet and gold as though someone were turning on colored lights.

Joey and Joan carried a few more buckets of water to the thirsty vegetables, and the professor lit his pipe.

"I wonder," said Mrs. Brown thoughtfully, "why they call it Cricket Creek when we've never heard a cricket."

"I think you will a little later in the summer," said the professor.

All of a sudden it was twilight, then dark. There were a million stars in the sky, but tonight there was no moon. They didn't need one, Joan decided. Out here above Cricket Creek the stars gave enough light. It was soft and soothing and sort of comforting. Problems didn't seem so big or unsurmountable in the friendly glow of the stars.

"Time for bed," said Mrs. Brown at last, getting to her feet.

The professor had already retired to his tent. He always turned in early, since he was up every morning before the sun.

For once the twins made no protests. Neither pleaded that he was not sleepy, or asked for a last drink of water from the well, or remembered something he had forgotten to do during the day which simply must be attended to before bedtime. They said good night and went to their own rooms, quietly closing the doors behind them. But, once they were there, neither undressed or got into bed.

Fortunately Mrs. Brown always slept with her door open. This was so that, in case one of the children was ill during the night and called to her, she would hear instantly. The twins knew this, and inside their own rooms each crouched on the floor with an ear to the large, old-fashioned keyhole. The moment the sound of her breathing grew louder and more regular, two doors opened simultaneously.

They did not speak, but, walking on tiptoes with a careful regard for old, squeaking boards, they passed down the hallway, through the kitchen, and into the outside darkness.

"Come over to the far side of the house," whispered Joey. "We don't want to wake the professor either."

Joan nodded and followed her brother as he crossed the yard to where the dirt road straggled down the slope.

"He may not come by the road," she whispered. "The way he gets around, he probably wouldn't bother with it."

"We've got to wait somewhere," Joey reminded her. "This is as good a place as any."

They did not have long to wait. It seemed that they were there no time at all before George came padding toward them. He followed the road after all, and in the starlight he seemed bigger and more awesome than ever.

"My dear friends," he greeted them enthusiastically. "Are you waiting to thank me? I assure you it wasn't necessary. It was a pleasure. A real pleasure."

"What was a pleasure?" asked Joey.

"Why, eating your sagebrush, of course. I enjoyed every minute of it. Don't thank me at all. It's I who should thank you."

"George," interrupted Joan earnestly, "we want you to do something for us. We want to ask a favor."

"Ask it. Ask it," urged George. "What are friends for, except to grant favors?"

Suddenly the stegosaurus broke off speaking. He lifted his head as though listening to something, and the spiked tail became motionless.

"Strangers," he said. "There are strangers in those caves, and one of them is stirring. Instinct tells me to go. You must excuse me."

With a quick motion, almost unbelievable in a creature that size, he whirled about and started back up the road the way he had come.

"George!" protested Joey in surprise.

"Wait, George," called Joan, forgetting to be quiet. She started running after the stegosaurus. "Wait for me and we'll go somewhere where we can talk. I just have to talk to you, George. You have to help me."

Joey suddenly realized he was being left alone. He struck out up the road after the others.

Chapter Six

AT THE TOP OF THE HILL Joan's entreaties seemed to
have an effect on the stegosaurus. He slackened his
speed and finally stopped to wait for her. But he was still
nervous. The bright, black eyes glittered in the starlight
as the creature turned his head from side to side. The
beaklike mouth opened and closed, and the long tail
seemed to droop behind the massive legs, the four sharp
spikes bristling dangerously.

Joey came panting and puffing up the final grade.

"George," he gasped reproachfully. "Are you afraid?"

"No," denied George. "Why should I be afraid? Allosaurus, the great hunter, could not hurt me. He tried,
and his enormous jaws and daggerlike teeth slipped
off my armor plate and could not get through. Tyrannosaurus Rex tried to hold me in his iron grip, as he
did Brontosaurus and the other thunder lizards. I slashed
him open with the spikes on my tail. If I am not afraid
of these two most terrible creatures who ever walked, I
do not know what fear is."

"But you ran, just because you heard Professor Harris
turn over in his sleep."

"I am shy," explained the stegosaurus with dignity. "There is a difference between being shy and being afraid."

"Of course there is." Joan looked at Joey angrily. "But now that we're up here, and there's no danger of the professor hearing us and waking up, we can talk, can't we?"

"If you're very sure he won't follow," agreed George after a moment. "Instinct will tell me if he comes out of his cave, so if I am suddenly forced to leave, you won't try to stop me again?"

"I promise," said Joan.

"Listen, George," began Joey impatiently. "Do you know where we can find any footprints of dinosaurs on the rocks?"

"Footprints? Of dinosaurs? On the rocks?" repeated George carefully. "I have told you I am the only one left. Do you mean my footprints?"

"No, no," said Joan. "Joey, I wish you'd let me ask this in my own way. You're only confusing him."

"So easy to do," sighed George. "You see, I have such a small — "

"I know," interrupted Joan gently. "George, a long time ago, when there were other dinosaurs besides you, things were different around here, weren't they?"

"Oh, yes," agreed George instantly. "Very, very different. There was no sagebrush in those days. I ate something else then. But do you know, it's been so long ago I've forgotten what it was."

"And there was water. A lot of water?"

"I think so," agreed the stegosaurus, two wrinkles appearing between his beady eyes as he attempted to reconstruct the past. "Yes, there was water. How else could the giant thunder lizards feed? And, without water, how could the duckbill dinosaurs get away from the land dinosaurs who ate meat? They had no armor plate like mine. They could only swim. Yes, there was water. But it must have gone away."

"Were there special places, shallow places, where the dinosaurs walked?"

"You take too much time," accused Joey, but they did not seem to hear him. Joan was intent on trying to rebuild the stegosaurus' dim memory, and George was attempting to please her, straining the capacity of his brain to the utmost.

"There must have been," he agreed finally. "I remember the hump on Brachiosaurus' head bobbing along over the surface of water. He fed that way, you know. His nostrils were on the top of his head, and he would wade on the bottom, feeding on the soft vegetation, with only his nose sticking out."

"Didn't he ever come on land?" demanded Joey with interest.

"Oh, yes," agreed George carelessly. "All dinosaurs came on land sometimes. They had to, to lay their eggs."

"You mean dinosaurs lay eggs? Were you hatched from an egg?"

"Of course," said George. "Weren't you?"

"No," said Joey, shaking his head. "I wasn't."

"But these dinosaurs who fed in the water, or waded in it," persisted Joan, "do you remember where it was they did their wading?"

"Why, wherever there was water, of course."

"And where was the water?"

"Here. Somewhere. It must have been. But everything has changed so. Then there were shallow seas and rivers. There were trees, but no grass. It was warm. Even the rain was warm. There were no rocks, no sagebrush."

"When did they come?" demanded Joey.

"How do I know?" said George. "I awoke once from a very long sleep, and they were here. Everything was as it is now. And I was all alone. I was the only one left."

His head sank lower toward the ground, and a harsh, rasping sound came from his throat. The twins realized with dismay that the stegosaurus was sobbing.

"But you aren't forgotten," said Joan hastily. "You dinosaurs are still remembered, George. People are interested in you. Why, they're even interested in the places where your ancestors and their friends walked."

"Really?" said George, and the rasping sound stopped. "That's very friendly of them. If I just weren't so shy — But, of course, I am, and there's nothing to be done about it."

"You don't have to do anything," soothed Joan, "except remember a little."

"I think I have done remarkably well remembering already," said George a little huffily.

"Oh, you have. You've done fine. We just want you to remember where the shallow water was. The places where they waded."

"Places where the water dried up sometimes," explained Joey, "and there was only mud for a while. Then the water came back."

"You ask too much of me," wailed George. "Even with your huge brains, I doubt if you could remember such things after all this time. And since they walked everywhere, the land dinosaurs on land, the water dinosaurs in water, what does it matter? You can pick out almost any spot you please, and you'd probably be right."

"But we have to find a footprint," said Joan patiently. "When something steps in mud and leaves a footprint, and the mud dries, then the water comes up again, it sometimes turns into stone. Only the stone has the exact shape of the footprint still on it. It's like a picture of that thing. Now do you understand?"

"I'm trying," said George earnestly. "I'm trying very hard to understand. You mean that somewhere about this place is a rock with the picture of a dinosaur's foot on it?"

"That's it!" They both cried out together. "Do you know where one is?" added Joey quickly.

"What would men do with it if they found one?" asked George cautiously.

"Why, they'd take it up, the whole rock, and put it in a museum. A museum is a big building — a cave — filled with all kinds of wonderful things," said Joan. "And peo-

ple would come from miles and miles to look at the picture on the rock. And they'd say, 'Just look how big that dinosaur's foot was. What a gigantic creature he was! No animal today is half so big.' And they'd go back home and tell all their friends what they'd seen."

"How nice." George nodded. "How nice and friendly. And the people wouldn't even come here to look at the picture? They'd carry it away, and strangers would go someplace else to see it?"

"Of course."

"That settles it," announced the stegosaurus. "It's a great tribute, and it will be a comfort to me in my loneliness to know that everyone is admiring a picture of my ancestor's foot. I'll help you."

"You mean you'll show us where one is?" cried Joey.

"Oh, no," said George. "I don't know that. I mean I'll help you look."

"Well, so much for your idea," scoffed Joey to his sister. "I can't see that it turned out any better than mine."

"Of course it will," she insisted. "Because something may come back to him. He may know the right places to look in."

"When shall we start?" demanded George. "Perhaps we'd better start right now, before we forget what we're looking for."

"I don't think we should start now," objected Joan. "Not till daylight, anyway. We couldn't see very well."

"I can see perfectly," said George, turning his head from side to side. "I can't imagine what is wrong with your eyes that you can't."

"They just don't work so well after dark," said Joan meekly.

"Too bad," sympathized the stegosaurus. "We all have our misfortunes. You have your eyes, I have my brain."

"But if you want to start tonight, it's all right with us," put in Joey hastily. "We don't mind you getting a head start."

"How generous of you," said George gratefully. "But then we are friends, so it's no wonder you're generous. Very well, then. I'll begin right away. As soon as I've had my lunch, of course."

"And we'll be up to the rocks as early as we can after sunup," promised Joan.

The stegosaurus looked at them each in turn, wagged his tail rapidly, then turned and ambled off to the rocky pinnacles which were his home.

The twins were up early the next morning. Ordinarily Mrs. Brown prepared the professor's breakfast, and he was away on his daily fossil search long before the children were out of bed. She had only poured the coffee, however, when Joan appeared, with Joey close on her heels.

"Well," said the professor in some surprise. "What brought this on?"

"We thought we'd go help hunt for footprints in the rocks," explained Joan.

Mrs. Brown looked dubious.

"But Mom, it isn't hot yet," argued Joan. "It won't start to get hot until way into the morning. Look, the sun isn't even up. If we went out now and came back early, you shouldn't worry about it."

"Professor Harris won't want to leave his own work just to bring you two back early."

"He won't have to," explained Joey. "We'll take Daisy Belle. Besides, we shouldn't all look in the same place. It would be better to scatter out. We'll take the rocks closer to home, and he can look where he has been looking. Or on beyond that."

"I am touched," said the professor. "Really touched by the children's desire to help in my work. I prophesy a great future for them. Perhaps they'll become scientists."

"Well, I don't know about that," said Mrs. Brown doubtfully. "But it is educational. And if we aren't going to be here ourselves much longer — "

"Mom!" protested both twins at the same time.

"Now, now," she said. "You've had a nice vacation, but you know as well as I do that it won't work out once winter comes."

"There's a school bus," argued Joey. "It picks up kids around here."

"That's enough, Joey!" Mrs. Brown used the special tone which meant that the subject was closed. However, at sight of their woebegone faces she relented a little. "It's going to have to come, and you both know it. But there's no reason why you should spoil the rest of your time here thinking about it. You may go help the professor look for fossils until it starts to get hot."

They finished breakfast, and the professor started up his car, which made so much noise that the twins had privately agreed it must be as old as George. He waved them a jaunty good-by and started puffing and toiling up the road while Joey was still putting the blanket on Daisy Belle.

"Do you suppose George found anything?" asked Joey finally, putting into words the single thought they had both shared since last night.

"Oh, I hope so," said Joan, crossing her fingers. "He's just got to."

George appeared almost before the echo of their voices died away against the rocks. He had been waiting for them, and they had never seen him so excited. He wiggled all over like a puppy, and the triangular plates of horn up and down his back seemed to quiver with delight.

"Oh, my friends," he called, his voice shrill and piping with enthusiasm. "I thought you'd never come. I was afraid you'd never get here."

"You mean — " began Joan fearfully. It was almost too much to hope for, and she was afraid to put her question into words.

"Did you find one?" demanded Joey, who had no such fears.

But George was not to be put off so casually. He had

73

been stirred out of the monotony of his daily existence, and he was determined to let them know exactly how he felt.

"I've had such fun!" he declared. "I could hardly take time to eat, it was so exciting. Like a game, you know, only you don't need anyone to play it with you. You can play it all by yourself. Why, if I had just had the brains to think of it, I could have been playing it for years. There wouldn't have been time to be lonely."

"What are you talking about?" demanded Joey sharply. "We asked you to look for a picture of a dinosaur's foot on a rock. Did you find one?"

"Well, not exactly," said George. "But I found something. I'm getting warm. And that's the exciting part of the game, isn't it?"

"What did you find? A dinosaur bone?"

"I told you how I feel about that," said George stiffly. "Besides, that wouldn't be part of the game at all. I wasn't looking for bones. I was looking for rock pictures. And I found one."

"Of what?" shouted Joey.

"Where is it, George?" said Joan, hardly able to breathe with excitement. A rock picture had to be a fossil. It couldn't be anything else, not unless it had been painted on or carved out by man.

"It's close to my hidden river," said George. "Follow me."

Once again they made the tortuous climb up slopes and down slides, staying as close as they dared to the dangerously wagging tail. George arrived there well ahead of them, and they found him standing proudly over something on the ground.

"Don't turn it over yet," said George. "The picture is on the other side, but before you look I want to tell you how I found it."

"It looks as though someone had been digging around here," observed Joey curiously. "There are big holes in the ground, and the earth is all broken up. I noticed it the first time we came, but it's worse today."

"I have," agreed George promptly. "And that's the way I found the picture. You see, I get very little chance to use the spikes on my tail these days. My enemies have been vanquished long ago, so I'm in constant danger of them growing dull. I shouldn't like that to happen, so I often sharpen them, like this."

He turned sideways, and the long tail threshed wildly, the spikes striking and grinding against the hard soil. The twins stepped hastily back out of the way as clods and small bits of rocky soil flew up from the attack.

"You sure stir up a mess," observed Joey.

"Exactly," agreed George. "That's why I'm careful to do the sharpening only in this place instead of in the open where people can see."

"That's really using your brain," admired Joey.

"Thank you so much," said George. He left off with his tail threshing. "When anything disturbs me, I always sharpen my tail. It has a soothing effect. And I will admit now that I was just a little upset at that stranger stirring

75

in his cave last night. When I left you, I came straight here and decided to calm my nerves with a little tail sharpening. Almost at once I struck something hard. I knew it was a rock. 'A rock,' I said to myself. 'That is what you are looking for.' So I looked at it. And there it was. I have won the first game."

"May we see it now?" asked Joan.

"Go right ahead," urged George.

The rock was not large, and Joey turned it over easily. There on the surface was the perfect impression of a bushy twig. They could make out the small leaves, even to the veins in them.

"Aren't you pleased?" demanded George. "It's a rock picture."

"But not the rock picture we wanted," objected Joan.

"Well, of course, it isn't as pretty as a dinosaur's foot," agreed George. "But it's something a dinosaur might eat. At least I'd try to eat it if it weren't stone. And I really think I did well, considering it's the first time I played this game."

"Oh, you did, George," Joan assured him. "Very well indeed. And I hope you'll keep on playing."

"I will," promised George. "It's great fun. Let's all play. It makes it more interesting to have more than one in the game."

Chapter Seven

GEORGE GENEROUSLY GAVE his rock picture to them, and the children carried it home when they went.

"Maybe the professor will buy it," suggested Joey tentatively. "Even if it's not a dinosaur, it's a fossil."

But the professor said nothing about purchasing the plant fossil when he returned home after another fruitless search of his own.

"It's a nice little specimen with which to start your collection," he said. "And it is a genuine fossil, although I doubt if it's very old."

"How can you tell?" demanded Joey.

The professor picked up the rock and studied it intently.

"The plant, whatever it is, would not be foreign to this climate as we know it now. I'm not a botanist, so I can't be sure, but it looks suspiciously like sagebrush."

"But sagebrush hasn't been here long enough to make a fossil!"

"If the conditions are right, and there is a great deal of mineral in the soil, a fossil can be made in only a few hundred years," explained the professor. "True, there must have been a great amount of mineral to turn such a comparatively new plant like sagebrush into one. Usually, of course, it takes thousands of years. But, if your dog buries a bone in the right place, it could turn into a fossil for your grandchildren or great-grandchildren to dig up."

"Nuts," said Joey in disgust.

The week was passing rapidly. Every morning the twins struggled out of bed the moment they heard the professor's voice in the kitchen. They finished their breakfasts almost as fast as he, and by the time he was preparing to start out in his old car, Joey was readying Daisy Belle. Mrs. Brown agreed that, so long as they returned before the heat of the day, they could go to the rocks every morning.

So far their search had been unsuccessful. Even George was not finding any more rock pictures, for the plant fossil had been his first and last. He was not so enthusiastic as he had been in the beginning. Fossil hunting at night interfered with his eating, and, as he assured the twins earnestly, he had to eat enough all summer to last him during the long winter's sleep.

There was very little sagebrush left about the ranch house now. Mrs. Brown noticed it but only looked sad and said nothing. She thought the twins were clearing it out in order to prove to her how industrious they were. She wished they could stay on the ranch to which her children seemed so attached, but without money coming in she knew it was impossible.

One morning Daisy Belle seemed so listless and unwilling to start forth on her morning jaunt that the twins did not have the heart to make her go.

"Let's walk," suggested Joey. "We've done it before."

"All right," agreed Joan. "The poor old thing needs a rest. If she only knew we were doing this partly for her, she'd feel different. I just don't know what will happen to Daisy Belle when we leave."

George was waiting for them when they arrived, but today he didn't want to look for rock pictures.

"Let's play a new game," he said. "I'm tired of this old one. I can't see what fun it is if you can never win."

"But maybe you will win today," said Joan. "Maybe this is the day when you'll find a dinosaur-foot picture."

"I don't think so," argued George. "I'm all stirred up today. My instincts are all aquiver. I feel as though something were about to happen."

"Good or bad?" asked Joey quickly.

"I don't know. I'm just too jumpy to tell."

"Well, let's go down to your hidden river," said Joan soothingly. "You always like it there, and that's where you found the fossil. Joey and I can hunt, and you can just watch if you'd rather."

"A splendid idea," agreed George. "I'll sharpen my tail. I always sharpen it when I'm disturbed about something. It makes me feel better."

"Good," said Joey cheerfully. "Maybe you'll uncover something again."

When they reached the spring, however, George was out of the mood for sharpening his tail. He had a long drink of the scalding water, then just stood with his small head drooping lower than usual. Certainly the stegosaurus was in an unhappy frame of mind. Except when one of them spoke to him directly, the formidable tail remained motionless. Even then it seemed to manage only a brief and feeble wag.

Joey and Joan went about their search as they had seen the professor do. They examined the lower slopes of the rocky walls. They kicked at the biggest clods of earth dug up by George when he had sharpened his tail. Suddenly George lifted his head, and the horned shields along his spine seemed to bristle in anger.

"Get back against the cliff!" he ordered. "Flatten yourselves against it, so he can't see you."

Without stopping to ask why, they did as the stegosaurus told them. He himself came to stand against the rocks, and as usual his colors seemed to melt into theirs. He stood with his head raised, so that he could see the blue, cloudless ceiling of the sky, and without thinking the twins looked up too.

There, high above them, was an airplane. It seemed to be growing larger, and they realized it must be coming down. They could see the wings, and by listening hard they thought they even heard the sound of an engine. The plane seemed to be circling, as though the pilot might be making an observation.

"Why, it's only a plane," said Joey. "A little one, too.

Probably a private — "

"Sh!" said George quickly. "Get back against the rocks. I don't want him to see us, and he has keen eyes. I'm just not up to coping with his insults today."

As they watched, it became even more evident that the plane was preparing to land. It made a last circle, and the sound of the engine was, for a moment, a deafening roar. Then the side of the cliff above them shut off their view, and the noise ceased.

"He came awful close to those cliffs," worried Joan.

"He'd have to," said George grimly. "He has to hook his claws on a rock or a branch when he wants to rest. He doesn't walk, you know. He can't get off the ground once he's on."

"Who can't? What are you talking about?" demanded Joey.

"Why, Pteranodon, of course!"

"What's a Pteranodon?"

"You just saw him," said George sharply.

The children had never seen their friend in such an irritable mood, and they looked at each other in amazement.

"You mean that airplane that just went over?" asked Joey cautiously.

"You may call it what you like," said George. "But the name won't improve its mean, nasty disposition or its bragging, swaggering manner. It's still a Pteranodon, and I hate it."

"You shouldn't hate anything, George," said Joan reproachfully. "I didn't think you did. I thought you were just shy."

"I am," said the stegosaurus after a moment. "And I suppose that's why I hate them. When they insult me — and they always do — I can never think of anything to say back until it's too late. And, of course, that doesn't do any good, so I have my feelings hurt. You remember I have sensitive feelings, don't you?"

"I remember," Joan nodded.

"But what can an airp — I mean a Pteranodon say to insult you?" puzzled Joey.

"They tease me about my little brain," confessed George. "They have big ones, you know. All the Pterodactyls do."

"Pterodactyls?"

"The Pteranodons belong to the Pterodactyl family of dinosaurs," explained George. "That means they have wings and can fly. There are all kinds of them. Some have long tails, and some don't have any. And some fly when it's dark and others only when it's daylight. But they all have bigger brains than the rest of us, and they all boast about it. Pteranodon brags the loudest because he's biggest."

"Oh, George," said Joan quickly. "That wasn't a flying dinosaur. That was just a machine."

"I don't know what a machine is."

"Well, it's something made by men to do their work for them."

"What is work?"

"Work is something you have to do, because if you don't you can't have something else that you do want."

"You don't need to try to explain that to me," said the stegosaurus after a moment. "I know I shouldn't understand it."

"I don't think he would either," Joey said. "He's got everything he wants without working for it. But, George, I wish you'd believe us that that wasn't a flying dinosaur, and that he wouldn't insult you if he met you face to face."

"I can't believe you," said George firmly. "Every time I see a Pteranodon gliding up in the sky I grow so angry I can hardly restrain myself. For a long time they went away. I was beginning to think that they, like the other dinosaurs, were all gone. And then one day not so long ago, perhaps a couple of dozen sleeps ago, they began to reappear. There weren't many. The sky isn't filled with them as it used to be, but every once in a while one glides over. I always hide. I just can't stand to have my feelings hurt again."

"How about birds?" said Joey thoughtfully. "There are some of them around. Eagles and buzzards and so on."

"Oh, those!" said George scornfully. "No one would mistake a bird for a flying dinosaur. Birds have feathers. Pterodactyls don't."

It was some time before George would allow them to leave their place of concealment against the rocks, but when the plane did not reappear he finally agreed they could resume their search for fossils. He himself sharpened the spikes on his tail, and the earth fairly flew as the sharp blades struck again and again. A great, yawning hole appeared only a little distance from the bubbling mineral spring.

"It's funny he doesn't uncover any more rocks than he does," said Joey.

"That may be one reason why he picks this place," said Joan wisely. "The ground is hard, but the soil goes down a long way. Maybe rocks would just dull the spikes instead of sharpening them."

"How about a whetstone, silly?" said Joey in a superior tone.

At last they could tell by the position of the sun that it was time to go. The morning had raced by before they knew it. George accompanied them to the other side of the ridge. His workout had done him good, and much of his restlessness and ill-humor was gone.

"Tonight I plan to finish off the rest of your sagebrush," he told them proudly. "I've had a fine time and enjoyed every mouthful."

"Thank you," said Joan.

Joey said nothing. There was no need in confessing to George that his efforts had been in vain. If they had to leave the ranch and go back to town, Joey couldn't bring in prospects to inspect the fine job of clearing done on their own land. There would be no need of soliciting business if he himself weren't there to collect the money. George might as well eat sagebrush wherever it happened to grow.

Joey was in the lead, with Joan following close behind, and George, chattering away as though to make make up for lost time, ambling along behind her. As they reached the last summit, Joey stopped.

"Look!" he cried, pointing down to the plain below.

There on the brown earth, a few hundred yards from the bottom of the cliffs, sat the plane they had seen earlier that morning. It was a small one, built for only two passengers, and it had been brought to a neat and safe landing on the level ground. The sun glittered on the metal, but there were no signs of life about it. The pilot had landed, then for some reason or other had gone away and left it sitting there.

"Now what — " began Joey in amazement. He stopped short as he felt himself pushed rudely out of the way.

With a shrill scream George had rushed forward. He, too, had seen the defenseless plane and, forgetting his shyness, was rushing forth to do battle. All the many re-membered insults of his old enemy, Pteranodon, sud-denly echoed about his ears. He remembered the many occasions when the flying dinosaur had glided just out of reach, hurling boasts and disparaging remarks. The stegosaurus hadn't been able to reach Pteranodon then, but he could reach him now, for without an air current to help, flying dinosaurs could not get off the ground.

Joan realized what was happening first.

"George!" she screamed. "George, come back! That isn't a flying dinosaur. It's only a machine."

"Jumping Jerusalem!" cried Joey. "We've got to stop him. Come on, Joan."

They hurried as fast as they could down the last slope and out onto the dusty expanse which stretched between the cliffs and the road, but they were too late. George had already reached the plane. They saw him take up a stand parallel with the front end, then the tail lashed sideways. Again and again it struck, the sharp spikes digging deep, denting metal, then ripping it so that the front of the plane seemed to buckle, then come apart.

"George!" called Joey sharply as they came panting up. "Stop it! Stop it this minute!"

George stopped. The giant tail, which a moment before had been an instrument of destruction, began to waggle in the friendly fashion they knew so well.

"Did you see me?" demanded the stegosaurus. "Wasn't I splendid? Wasn't I magnificent? Oh, I tell you it will be a long time before another Pteranodon dares to say anything to me again. I showed this one. I really did. Without an air current his big brain does him no good. He's nothing. Nothing at all."

"Oh, George," said Joan helplessly. "Don't you know what you've done? That wasn't a Pteranodon at all. That was an airplane. It belonged to somebody who went away and left it here. And now you've wrecked it so it can't fly."

George walked over and sniffed the metal sides delicately.

"It's a Pteranodon all right," he told them triumphantly. "It hasn't any feathers."

Chapter Eight

ALL THE WAY BACK to the ranch house the children worried about what they would say if anyone asked them about the plane.

"I think we can tell the truth but not quite all of it," said Joey. "We can say we saw the plane come over and later on we saw it on the ground. And if they ask if it was broken when we saw it, we can say yes. Because, when we saw it last, it was broken."

"What if they should say 'the first time you saw it'?" worried Joan.

"Well, the first time we saw it, it was up in the air. I think they're more apt to ask if we saw any suspicious-looking characters hanging around."

"There's George."

"But we promised we wouldn't even speak about him. All we have to say is we didn't see any strange men around the plane on our way home. That's certainly the truth."

"What if we do, though?" Joan shivered. "See them on the way home, I mean. What if we meet the men who own the plane coming back to get it?"

Joey looked around a little apprehensively.

"Well, we haven't seen them so far," he said loudly. "I guess it's just a chance we have to take."

They met no strangers on the way home, but when they arrived, two men they did not know were sitting in the kitchen. Mrs. Brown looked up, smiling, as the children arrived.

"Oh, there you are," she said. "I was beginning to worry. The sun's starting to get hot."

"It's not really hot yet," said Joan. She looked at the two men a little fearfully.

"These are my children whom I told you about," introduced Mrs. Brown. "This is Joey, and this is Joan. This is Mr. Smith and Mr. Jones. They were flying over and ran out of gas. Luckily there was plenty of level ground to land on, and they walked along the road to the house."

"We saw the plane," said Joan.

"Yes. It seems to be broken," said Joey boldly.

The taller of the two men, Mr. Jones, laughed.

"Oh, it'll run okay as soon as we take on a little gas," he said. "If this professor your mother's been telling us about ever gets home, we'll get him to run us into town after some."

Mr. Smith smiled at the children a little nervously.

"Your mother says you were looking for fossils on the rocks," he said. "Did you find any?"

"No," answered Joan.

"I used to hunt sea shells when I was a small boy," said

Mr. Smith. "I guess it's about the same thing."

The twins smiled politely and regarded the two men with curiosity. It was a little frightening to be looking at someone who was soon to be faced with a great catastrophe but didn't know it was going to happen.

Mr. Jones was the younger of the two, and they decided he must have been the pilot of the plane. He was a big man, and his nose was a little crooked, as though it had once been broken and hadn't mended properly. He wore a leather jacket and under it a pink shirt, open at the collar. On his left hand he wore a large gold ring.

Mr. Smith was small, and his skin was pale. He had nearsighted eyes behind gold-rimmed spectacles, and he wore a neat, although drab, gray suit and a blue-and-gray necktie with a small design. He occupied one of the two rocking chairs in the kitchen, the one that always squeaked. It kept up a constant little succession of sounds as he rocked back and forth.

"Where were you going when you had to land?" asked Joey.

"To L.A.," said Mr. Jones, as though there was some doubt about it. "Mr. Smith hired me to fly him out, but we ran out of gas."

Mr. Smith looked at Mr. Jones severely.

"Don't you worry," said Mr. Jones quickly. "I'll get you there safe and sound all right. I always keep my word. You just leave everything to me, Mr. Smith."

"I hope so, Frank," said Mr. Smith in a troubled voice. "But I don't like delays. That's why I hired you to fly me

out, so I wouldn't be dependent on the planes of some airline."

"It'll be all right," soothed Mr. Jones. "We'll make it up when we get going. We were lucky to find a place like this to land."

"I think you're right," agreed Mr. Smith after a moment. "Since we had to run into difficulties, we were lucky to put down in this place. It's quiet here. Quiet and peaceful."

The rocking chair went squeak, squeak, squeak.

"It's quiet all right," agreed Mr. Jones, and from his tone they could tell he did not approve of quiet. He turned to Mrs. Brown. "You said you had a horse. I wish you'd let the kid ride into town and see if he can't round up somebody to bring us out some gas."

"No." Mrs. Brown shook her head firmly. "I don't want either of the children out in the hottest part of the day. They were out in it once, and I'm sure they must have had a slight stroke. They came back with the wildest tales."

Mr. Jones looked disappointed, but Mr. Smith only smiled sympathetically.

"But if one of you would like to take Daisy Belle and ride in, I'm sure you're welcome to her," added Mrs. Brown.

"Go ahead if you want to, Frank," said Mr. Smith with a strange little smile.

"No," said Mr. Jones hastily. "Me and horses don't hit it off somehow. I'll wait here with you, Mr. Smith. We'll ride in with the professor when he comes."

Mrs. Brown arose and began to get things ready for lunch. Joan got up, too, to help. She felt a little uncomfortable in the presence of these owners of the wrecked plane. She wondered what they would say when they saw it. What would they do? Of course, no one would suspect that the damage had been done by a stegosaurus, but someone might insist on a search of the rocky cliffs and jagged hills. George might be discovered in spite of himself, and then they would shut him up in a zoo somewhere. He wouldn't be happy in captivity. He might even die.

"Move the gentleman's brief case," said Mrs. Brown, "and set the table, Joan."

On the center of the square table where they always ate breakfast and lunch was a brown leather brief case. It must have been tightly packed, for the sides bulged a little. Joan turned to obey her mother, but Mr. Smith was before her. He picked up the brief case and smiled apologetically all around.

"I just don't know what's come over me," he exclaimed. "Leaving my things around in people's way!"

"You must have a lot in it," said Joey frankly. "It looks stuffed."

"It's filled with important papers," explained Mr. Smith. "Everything I have for this business trip is in here. It was hard to collect some of these papers too. Took a lot of time. I don't think I'd ever be able to do it again." He sat back down in the rocking chair and held the brief case in his lap. Then he turned to Joey. "Don't you ever get lonesome around here? I don't imagine you have much company."

"No, sir," said Joey. "We don't get lonesome. There isn't much company, but there's always something to do."

"I'm sure there must be," agreed Mr. Smith. "Someday I may buy a little place like this myself. I've often thought of it. A place a long way removed from everyone, where I can do exactly as I like without having to answer to anyone."

"You can still do that without being stuck way out in the sagebrush somewhere," objected Mr. Jones.

Joey glared at him. He didn't like people who didn't approve of the ranch on Cricket Creek.

"Ah, but the peace, Frank. Peace of mind, and the knowledge that you are master of all you survey," said Mr. Smith. "However, you can do as you like. As soon as you have delivered me to my destination I shall make no further calls on your services."

Both men ate everything Mrs. Brown served them for lunch, and when they had finished, Mr. Smith insisted on paying for the meal. He took a five-dollar bill from his wallet and presented it with a flourish.

"I'm not sure I have change." Mrs. Brown hesitated. "Haven't you anything smaller?"

"I don't want any change," said Mr. Smith. "We've put you out too much as it is, occupying your kitchen all day. Besides, it's been a long time since I ate home cooking. The meal was worth every cent. Don't you agree, Frank?"

Mr. Jones said nothing. He was watching as Mrs. Brown removed the lid from the cookie jar and dropped the bill down with their other money. There was something in his eyes that made Joey gulp in alarm.

What in the world had made his mother so careless? Joey knew, of course, that the gesture had been done without thinking. Every week, when the professor paid his board, Mrs. Brown opened the cookie jar and added the money to the five hundred dollars in savings already there. It didn't matter about the professor seeing. Anybody could tell that he was perfectly honest. It probably wouldn't matter about Mr. Smith, either. Joey had seen the edges of many bills in the wallet when Mr. Smith took out the five dollars. He was an important businessman with enough money to charter a private plane to fly him to the West Coast. Mr. Smith wouldn't be concerned with the small amount in the cookie jar. Mr. Jones might. In fact, Joey could read on the pilot's face that Mr. Jones was.

Joey didn't like that look. He wasn't sure Mr. Jones could be trusted. If there had been any way of getting Mrs. Brown aside, he would have asked her to take the money out of the cookie jar that minute and hide it somewhere else. He couldn't hide it himself. Not with all of them in the same room, watching.

There was nothing to do after lunch, so the twins went out to the barn, as they usually did in the afternoons.

"Do you know what I think?" said Joey, the moment they were out of earshot.

"No. What?"

"I think Mr. Jones is a crook."

"A crook!" Joan stopped short in her tracks and stared at her brother. "Joey Brown, if this isn't the silliest thing you've thought of yet."

"It isn't silly at all. Did you see him watch Mom when she put the money Mr. Smith gave her in the cookie jar?"

"No." Joan stopped arguing, and her face grew serious. "What did he do?"

"He didn't do anything. He just looked. And it was the way he looked that gave him away. He wanted that money."

"Oh, dear," worried Joan. "He'll want it more than ever when he sees what's happened to his plane. I'll bet it will take a lot of money to get it fixed up."

"I wish Mom wouldn't keep her money there," fumed Joey. "Everybody knows banks are where you're supposed to keep money."

"She's going to," said Joan. "Don't you remember, when she took the money out of the bank at home, she said she'd put it in the bank at Silo right away? Only there wasn't any bank when we got here. Silo's too little. People go on to the next town to do their banking, and we just haven't been that far yet."

"Well, what are we going to do about it?"

"You'll have to tell Mom," decided Joan. "Tell her you saw Mr. Jones watching — and how he looked. She'll have to hide it someplace else."

Joey agreed, and when Mrs. Brown came to the well

later in the afternoon he rushed out to intercept her and told her his suspicions. Mrs. Brown only laughed.

"Goodness, Joey," she said indulgently. "What an imagination you have. I'm afraid you saw too many movies and television programs. They put a lot of crazy ideas in your head."

"What did she say?" asked Joan, when he returned to the barn.

"She says I have too much imagination," reported Joey glumly.

"Well, maybe you have."

"And maybe I haven't too. It won't hurt to keep my eye on that cookie jar. And on Mr. Jones, either."

It was nearly dark when the professor returned, but Mr. Jones demanded that he drive them straight into Silo even before they had eaten dinner. Mr. Jones had been getting more impatient and edgy as the afternoon progressed. Joey had observed that he couldn't seem to sit still as Mr. Smith did. He seemed to be getting up, then sitting down, then coming outside, then going in again.

"I'm afraid gas won't do you any good," said Professor Harris, shaking his head. He had not had a chance to say anything before, except "How do you do," for Mr. Jones had immediately begun an account of their forced landing and the necessity of Mr. Smith's proceeding to Los Angeles to keep his business appointment.

"Of course it will," said Mr. Jones, and his tone suggested that the professor didn't know anything about planes.

"You can't fly with most of the engine smashed to pieces, can you?" asked the professor mildly.

"There's nothing wrong with the engine," bristled Mr. Jones.

"I'm afraid you're wrong," contradicted the professor. "I saw the plane as I was returning home, and drove out of my way to inspect it. I'm afraid there's a very great deal wrong with the engine. It looks as though it had been run into by a bulldozer."

"That's impossible!" cried Mr. Jones. "It was fine when we left it. All we needed was a little gas."

"Perhaps we'd better drive out and have a look at the plane, Frank," suggested Mr. Smith. He spoke calmly, but he seemed a little worried. He no longer smiled at the children, and two deep wrinkles of concentration appeared between his eyebrows.

"You'll eat first, won't you?" asked Mrs. Brown.

"No, no. I've got to see what's happened to my plane," cried Mr. Jones. "I've got to see it right now."

The professor sighed a little. He had spent a long, grueling day, and he was tired. But he must have understood Mr. Jones' anxiety, for he stood up.

"I'm sure it won't take long," he apologized to Mrs. Brown. "I'll drive as fast as I can."

Mrs. Brown put the dinner on the back of the stove after they had gone.

"What in the world could have happened to their

plane?" she wondered. "You told them it was broken, didn't you, Joey? But they didn't pay any attention to you."

"People ought to pay attention to me," he said quickly. "You'd better move the money from that cookie jar so Mr. Jones won't steal it."

"Mr. Jones has bigger things on his mind right now than money in someone else's cookie jar. Did either of you see any strangers when you were out there this morning?"

"No, Mother. We didn't see a single stranger," answered Joan honestly.

"It's certainly curious," mused Mrs. Brown. "Do you suppose it just exploded by itself in the sun? From the heat?"

"I don't think so," said Joan. "I don't think that's the way it happened at all."

Notwithstanding the professor's promise to hurry, it was a good hour before they returned. He looked more tired and exhausted than ever, and Mr. Jones was glum and silent, but Mr. Smith seemed to have recovered a little of his gentle good humor.

"The plane's a wreck," he told Mrs. Brown and the children, shaking his head. "Poor Frank! He thinks it's going to call for a whole new engine."

"Just when I got this one paid for, too." Mr. Jones scowled. "I don't know where I'm going to get the dough."

"Something will turn up," said Mr. Smith soothingly.

"I'm going to pay you for the whole trip, even though you didn't get me clear there."

"A drop in the bucket! I've got to dig up a lot more than that," groaned Mr. Jones. "What do you suppose happened? Who could have done a dirty trick like that?"

No one answered, and Mrs. Brown motioned them to take places around the table. Dinner was a little dry, but she had managed to keep it warm. Earlier the children had eaten slices of bread and jam which spoiled their appetites, and only Mr. Smith, it seemed, was hungry. Mr. Jones sat stirring at his food, and the professor's eyes kept closing and his head falling forward. Finally he jerked it up and gave it a little shake.

"Gentlemen," he apologized. "I don't know what I was thinking of. That three-o'clock bus through Silo is northbound. It wouldn't do you any good. It would land you up in Portland or Seattle. If you want the southbound for California, it doesn't go through until seven in the morning."

"Oh, dear," said Mr. Smith mildly. "Another delay." He looked reproachfully at Mr. Jones. "You should have kept closer watch on your gas tank, Frank."

"Now don't start panning me," said Mr. Jones angrily. "If you hadn't taken it in your head to change course half a dozen times on the way out, I'd have been able to take on gas as I intended to. It's not my fault at all. Now here I am, stuck out in the sagebrush with a busted plane, and — "

"Now, now," interrupted Mr. Smith hastily. "I didn't mean anything, Frank. Of course it's not your fault."

"I can't find a new engine and parts in a little jerk-water town like Silo," continued Mr. Jones. "I'll have to take the bus into some place bigger and then maybe wire the factory. If you think this is my idea of a good time — "

"We'll find some place for you to sleep here tonight," said Mrs. Brown, looking with sympathy at the drooping professor. "Joey — ?"

Joey knew that she was waiting for him to offer his room to the guests. There were three bedrooms in the ranch house, and it had seemed such luxury, everyone having a room of his own, that they had each taken one. He closed his lips tightly and avoided his mother's eyes. He wouldn't give up his room. Not to anyone he was sure had the tendencies of a thief.

"Joan can come in with me," decided Mrs. Brown after a moment. "And you may have her room."

"I wouldn't think of it," said Mr. Smith. "We'll sleep in the barn. I presume there is hay? It will be a little experience in roughing it, won't it, Frank? Sort of a lark."

"I've roughed it before," said Mr. Jones shortly. "But I'd like to get out of here. I've sat around twiddling my thumbs long enough."

The professor went to his tent immediately after dinner, and Mr. Jones and Mr. Smith retreated to the barn soon after. Everyone must get a good rest, Mr. Smith insisted genially, if they were to be up in time to catch the seven-o'clock bus.

Joey went to his room, but he had no intention of going to sleep. He intended to stay awake all night and keep an eye on the cookie jar. He wasn't going to give Mr. Jones, now that he was more desperate than ever for money, a chance to come in and rifle its contents.

He lay on his bed fully dressed and wide awake, thinking about Mr. Jones and the cookie jar. Suddenly he had a terrifying thought. Thieves were experienced. They could enter a house silently and creep about in the dark without being heard. Perhaps, even while he lay there, Mr. Jones was in the kitchen helping himself to their money.

There was only one thing to do. He must get the cookie jar and bring it into his own room for safekeeping. There were no keys for the locks, but he could put a chair under the doorknob, and no one could break in without being heard.

Stealthily he arose, managed to swing open the door without letting it squeak as it generally did, and crept down the hall into the kitchen. Faint light from the stars and a slice of moon which hung in the sky came through the window. He could make out the objects in the room clearly enough to avoid chairs and tables. The stars and moon would give light for a prowler too.

In the cupboard Joey had to grope for the cookie jar, but he found it. He felt the smooth sides against his hands and lifted it down. He didn't know why, but he had a sudden impulse to look inside. Something told him it should be done now and not put off until he returned to his room.

He removed the lid and peered in. It was too dark to see, so he put his hand inside. On every side and on the bottom his fingers ran over the smooth pottery surface. There was no money there. The cookie jar was empty.

Chapter Nine

JOEY STOOD THERE for a moment, wondering what he should do. The empty cookie jar came as no surprise. He had expected Mr. Jones to steal the money all the time. Perhaps he should arouse the professor, his mother, and possibly Mr. Smith. Joey couldn't imagine gentle, wealthy Mr. Smith tolerating a thief. How upset he would be when he discovered that he actually had one in his employ. That would make three adults and two children against one man. That ought to be enough.

Then he remembered that criminals always carried guns. Joey didn't know too much about guns, but he had heard about six-shooters. Six-shooters could be fired six times without reloading. If Mr. Jones was a good shot, and he very probably was, he could shoot three adults and two children and still have one bullet left over. It made the odds too great.

In the movies and on television, people always summoned the law in cases like this. The nearest law to any ranch should be the sheriff. Joey didn't think Silo was a large enough town to have a sheriff. There was only one general store, with a post office combined, a gas pump, a church, a district school, attended by children from the surrounding ranches and farms, and a big cooperative, where farmers who were lucky enough to have some water on their land brought their wheat crops. Still, Silo was a town. It said so on the map. And, being a town, it should have a law officer with firearms of some kind. There was only one thing to do. Joey must summon the law. He must do it now, before the criminal had an opportunity to dispose of his loot.

He put down the cookie jar quietly and stole outside. It was dark and very quiet. He had never known anything to be so quiet. It would have been a relief to hear the distant howling of a coyote, but even they were silent tonight. He looked a little wistfully toward the white outline of the professor's tent on the side of the house. Perhaps he should awaken the professor, after all, and tell him what he had discovered. The professor would drive him into Silo and assume the responsibility of summoning the law. Then Joey remembered how tired the professor had been at dinner, and he decided he had better do it himself.

He looked fearfully at the shadowy bulk of the sagging barn and the spidery outline of the rail fence surrounding it. Something he saw in the fenced enclosure made his resolve even more strong. Mr. Jones had shut Daisy Belle outside. Normally the barn doors were left open, and the old horse usually went inside after dark. But tonight she couldn't, because the doors were tightly closed. Mr. Jones must have been responsible for that cruel act. Certainly Mr. Smith would not begrudge an old horse her nightly shelter or her bed of hay.

Joey started forward, but in the middle of the yard he stopped. He had glanced apprehensively over his shoulder and had seen George coming down the road. The stegosaurus was returning to finish off the last of the sagebrush as he had promised.

Joey turned and went to meet George. In his relief to be able to talk with someone he knew, he forgot that George had been, in a way, responsible for the whole thing. If the stegosaurus hadn't mistaken the plane for a flying dinosaur, Mr. Jones would have regassed his plane and been out of here by this time. The contents of the cookie jar would have remained undisturbed.

"George," began Joey in a low voice. "Something terrible has happened. Something just awful."

"More strangers have come," said George instantly.

"Yes. And one of them is a bad man. He's a thief!" Joey stopped, wondering how he could explain to George what the word meant. To his surprise, George understood.

"Oh!" said George indignantly. "The beasts! How many eggs did they steal?"

"Eggs?" repeated Joey stupidly.

"Certainly," said George. "Thieves are mammals. Generally they're little slinking furry things. And they steal the dinosaur's eggs. I don't think there's a worse trick in the world. I hate all mammals because of it."

"Man is a mammal," said Joey, almost without thinking.

"Man is different," said George. "He has two legs. I should have said I hate all four-footed mammals. They could be thieves."

"This thief is a man," Joey explained. "And he didn't steal eggs; he stole money."

"Money," repeated George. "I seem to remember you tried to tell me about that once before. Would you mind going over it again?"

"There isn't time," said Joey. "But you just take my word for it that it's important. And the man who stole our money is back there, sleeping in the barn."

George turned his head toward the shadowy bulk. He appeared nervous.

"But there's a chance I can get it back," continued Joey. "I'm going to ride into town and get help. The thief will have to stay here until morning. At seven he's going to catch a bus."

"Bus?" asked George.

"Never mind," said Joey hastily. "If I get help, we can get our money back before he gets away."

"Perhaps I should return another time," suggested George. "It seems there will be many strangers about. I could eat the sagebrush later."

"Oh, please don't. Please stay here until I come back with help," pleaded Joey. "You'll hear me coming. You always do, so there'll be plenty of time for you to get away. I'd feel better if I knew you were here. If the thief

tries to escape, you can follow and tell me where he goes."

"I don't know," objected George.

"Oh, please. We're friends, aren't we? And aren't friends supposed to help each other?"

"You're right," agreed George finally. "I'll stay until I hear you coming. And I'll watch that cave with the thieves in it every minute."

The stegosaurus retired toward the last patches of sagebrush, and Joey went to get old Daisy Belle. He led her out of the barnyard, past the house, and up the steep road, because he thought it would be more quiet that way. Daisy Belle required a great amount of clucking and many "giddaps" to keep her on a constant course. At the top of the hill he mounted and started down the road to Silo.

It was the first time Joey had ever gone to town alone, and the first time he had made the trip on horseback.

He was glad now that Daisy Belle had been allowed to rest that morning and was starting out fresh. He was sure she'd be able to make the trip into Silo and back, especially since it was cooler at night.

The whole country looked different to him. Perhaps it was because Daisy Belle traveled more slowly than a car, or perhaps it was because he was seeing it for the first time by starlight. Even the road seemed strange, filled with bends and little curves that he didn't remember seeing before. He wondered if it were the right road after all, but there was no other, so he kept Daisy Belle doggedly on her course, and after what seemed like many hours they reached Silo.

The little community was sleeping. It was as dark as the ranch on Cricket Creek, and Joey didn't know what he ought to do. He must wake someone up, of course, but who? Finally he decided on the house next to the store. It was occupied by Mr. Jaeggers, who ran the store and post office. Mr. Jaeggers would be the one to tell him who represented the law in Silo.

He tied Daisy Belle to a stunted tree in the yard and went up on the Jaeggers' porch. It was not so quiet in Silo as it had been on the ranch. The main highway ran straight through the middle of town, and occasional cars, with staring headlights, zoomed by. During the day they did not go so fast, as there was a sign along the road which read: ENTERING SILO. SPEED LIMIT 25 MILES. STRICTLY ENFORCED. At night most of the cars did not respect the warning, or perhaps they could not see it.

But Joey remembered the sign now, and it was a comforting thought. If Silo had someone to enforce speed laws, that same person should be qualified to apprehend a thief. He raised his hand and knocked discreetly on the front door.

Nothing happened. Another car thundered by and was gone. Joey knocked a little louder, then a little louder, until finally he was pounding on the door. Something happened then. An upstairs window directly above the porch roof grated open, and a man's disturbed voice came floating down.

"Who is it? What do you want?"

Joey stepped off the porch, away from the protecting roof, and looked up. Mr. Jaeggers' head was in the open window.

"It's me, Mr. Jaeggers. Joey Brown," said Joey politely. "Would you please tell me who's the sheriff in this town?"

"Sheriff?" said Mr. Jaeggers. His voice was a little husky because he had been awakened from a sound sleep, but Joey was relieved that he didn't seem to be angry about it. He only sounded surprised. "Ain't got no sheriff in Silo, Joey. What you want a sheriff for?"

"To catch a thief."

"You wait there," directed Mr. Jaeggers. "I better come down."

Joey went back and stood on the porch. After a few minutes Mr. Jaeggers opened the front door. He wore his trousers but no shirt, and his feet were bare.

"Come in, Joey," he invited. "You better tell me all about it, but talk fast. Your ma will be worried if you don't get back pretty quick."

"Mom doesn't know I'm here."

"You mean she don't know about the robbery?" said Mr. Jaeggers. "She didn't send you for the sheriff?"

"No. I thought of it myself."

"Oh," said Mr. Jaeggers, and his voice was a little disappointed. "Well, go on anyways. So long as you're here."

"Yesterday two men came to our house," began Joey.

"Their plane ran out of gas over by the cliffs east of the ranch. And Mom gave them lunch, and they paid her five dollars for it."

"A mighty hefty lunch," observed Mr. Jaeggers.

"Mom didn't want to take so much," explained Joey, flushing a little. "But they made her. And she put the money in the cookie jar where we keep our other money. And they saw her do it. They watched. And one of them looked kind of funny, like he'd like to have the money. Then tonight, when I felt in the cookie jar, it was empty. All the money was gone."

"Hm," said Mr. Jaeggers. "They probably took it, all right. The world is full of fellers with sticky fingers. How much was there?"

"I don't know exactly. But there were five hundred dollars in savings and all the money Professor Harris has been paying for board this summer."

"Land sakes!" exclaimed Mr. Jaeggers. "What's your ma thinking of, keeping all that money around?"

"Well, she was going to put it in the bank, only there isn't a bank in Silo," said Joey defensively.

"Then she should of put it in postal savings. It'd be safe there," said Mr. Jaeggers positively. He thought a moment before he asked, "You say they come in a plane? And run out of gas?"

"Yes."

"I wonder where they got more," said Mr. Jaegers speculatively. "My pump's the only one in town and the nearest one."

"Oh, they didn't get gas after all. When they went back to their plane it was wrecked. There's a big hole in the engine."

"How'd that happen?"

"They don't know who did it," said Joey. "They can't imagine. But the plane won't fly."

"Then how'd they get away?"

"They didn't. At least not yet. They're still sleeping in our barn. Professor Harris is going to drive them into Silo tomorrow to catch the bus."

"Well, now," said Mr. Jaeggers thoughtfully, "when they come in tomorrow maybe I better have a little talk with them. Before they leave town. After all, I'm the constable."

"You are?"

"Certainly." Mr. Jaeggers nodded. "'Twouldn't do no harm at all to talk to them. See what I can find out. What's their names?"

"Mr. Jones. He's the one. The one with him is Mr. Smith."

"Mr. Jones and Mr. Smith," repeated Mr. Jaeggers thoughtfully. "Now there's a real giveaway, Joey. I reckon you had the right hunch."

"What do you mean?"

"Why, their names, of course. They couldn't be real. That just about proves they're crooks. Mr. Jones *or* Mr. Smith I might go for. But Mr. Jones *and* Mr. Smith is mighty suspicious. Looks like they got something to hide."

"Oh, Mr. Smith isn't in on it at all," Joey assured him. "He's a nice man. He used to hunt sea shells when he was a little boy. But I wouldn't like to think what Mr. Jones did."

Mr. Jaeggers nodded agreement.

"You might as well stay the rest of the night, Joey," he invited. "It's a mighty long ride back to Cricket Creek. It won't seem so far by daylight. We got an extra bed."

"Oh no, thank you," said Joey quickly. "I'd better go back now. They don't know I'm gone, you see. Mom would be worried, and the professor might go out looking for me instead of driving Mr. Jones into Silo."

"That's right," agreed Mr. Jaeggers. "We don't want to do anything to make them suspicious. Now you just leave everything to me, Joey. I'll get back your money for you if they've got it. And then you tell your ma to put it in postal savings like I said."

"I will," promised Joey.

He went out into the night again to get Daisy Belle, who was still tied to the stunted tree but fast asleep on her feet. Mr. Jaeggers stood on his front porch and watched until they were out of town.

The way home didn't seem half so far as the trip there. Joey had too much to think about. He had never been so excited in his life. It was like playing a part on a television program. He was like the Cisco Kid or Matt Clark, Railroad Detective. Well, not exactly, either, for they brought in the prisoners themselves and delivered them to the police. Joey wouldn't be bringing in Mr. Jones at the point of a gun. But he was the one who had alerted the police. He wished Mr. Jaeggers had been a real sheriff instead of just a constable, but he guessed it was good enough.

From time to time Daisy Belle would stop still in the road, and Joey knew she was having a little rest. Usually she did this on hills, but the road to Silo was level and she did it anyway. Joey knew that it was her way of telling him she considered the trip too long for a horse of her years. He always let her rest a few moments before going on.

The rests were the only irritating part of the trip, for he was impatient to get home, and it was a little scary sitting up on Daisy Belle with the night all around him. Once he thought he heard a voice start to call his name. It got as far as "Jo — " and then it was shut off as though someone had turned the knob on a radio in the middle of a sentence. He peered all around, but he could see no one; only dark, rolling plains, scattered with darker blobs that were rocks or clumps of sagebrush, and a darker jagged line of rimrock along the north against the star-spattered sky. He didn't let Daisy Belle rest very long that time.

They had nearly reached Cricket Creek when he saw a car in the road ahead. There were the two yellow headlights coming straight toward him, and he pulled Daisy Belle off to the right before he realized the car wasn't moving. It was just sitting there.

Obviously some motorist was in trouble, and Joey was pleased that, since it had to happen, it had happened there. He would stop and ask if he could be of help. The inside of cars had a great fascination for him, and he never had enough opportunities to get under the hood.

As Daisy Belle came alongside, however, Joey saw there was no one in the car. He peered all round in the darkness and saw no one on the side of the road. Here was a real mystery indeed. If someone had run out of gas, Joey was sure they wouldn't walk away and leave the car lights burning. He knew that was hard on batteries. Unless, of course, they had just forgotten to turn them off.

Daisy Belle interpreted his order to "whoa" as an invitation to rest. She let her head droop, and Joey decided he might as well get down and investigate more fully. There was something about this abandoned car that seemed familiar.

Even before he looked in the back seat and saw the water bottle, the collection of picks and shovels, ropes and whisk brooms, he knew what it was. It was Professor Harris' car. No wonder it looked familiar. He had seen it in his own yard every night and morning since the professor had come seeking fossils. But what was it doing out here on the deserted road with its lights burning and no one around?

Perhaps the professor was out looking for him, Joey decided. Probably they had missed him after all, and a search party was scouring the neighborhood. There could be no other explanation. He raised his hand to his mouth to make a funnel.

"Hey!" he called. "Here I am. Over here by the car. It's me. Joey!"

"Joey?"

A voice answered him promptly from the darkness to his left, and an exceptionally large mass that he had taken to be sagebrush began to move. There was only one dry, inflectionless voice like that in the world.

"George!" cried Joey in amazement.

"Of course," agreed the stegosaurus, coming up beside the car.

Daisy Belle, whom they had always been careful to tie well out of sight of the creature, gave a wild, throaty bellow, reared on her old hind legs and galloped off down the road to the ranch house.

"Humph!" said George contemptuously. "Mammals!"

Chapter Ten

"WHAT ARE YOU DOING HERE?" demanded Joey. "And what is Professor Harris' car doing here too?"

"Is this called a car?" asked George, sniffing the back fender. "How my vocabulary is growing!"

"Answer my question," ordered Joey.

"Dear friend," said George earnestly, "I am here because I am keeping my promise to you."

"Your promise?"

"I promised you that if the thief escaped I would follow and tell you where he went. He did. And I did."

"But where is he?"

"The men disappeared. But this is the spot from which they disappeared. I am watching the spot, so if they reappear I can again follow."

"You'd better start at the beginning," said Joey helplessly. "I don't have the slightest idea what you're talking about."

"You will remember," began George promptly, "that when you left I was just starting to finish off the sagebrush."

"Yes."

"It was inferior," recalled George. "I have always relished the sagebrush which grew around your cave, but tonight it seemed to have lost its flavor. I think it was because the thought of so many strangers about upset my digestion."

"Go on with what happened," urged Joey. "Please go on."

"Very well," agreed George amiably. "But I should explain how my digestion was upset and how worried I was, or you'll never understand how I became so lax as to allow myself to be seen."

"Somebody saw you?"

"The thieves." George nodded. "There I was, nibbling away on my dinner, but worrying every minute for fear I might be surprised by one of the strangers. I was thinking about it so hard that it didn't seem strange at all when the entrance to the largest cave opened up and the two thieves came out. It was as though I were imagining the whole thing or dreaming it in a dream. It wasn't as though it were really happening."

"What did they do?"

"They seemed to be arguing about something. One of them seemed to want to do something, and the other agreed, but he wasn't sure it should be done right then. I gathered that he wanted to wait. Really, Joey, I was so upset I hardly heard what they said. I tell you it was exactly like a bad dream. And one can never remember all the conversation in a dream, can one?"

"I don't know," said Joey. "Then what?"

"Then they crossed the yard to where this thing you call a car was standing," continued George, with a shudder which shook each of the triangular shields along his spine. "And the worst happened!"

"What?"

"One of them turned around and saw me," admitted George. "They hadn't before. They had been too busy arguing to notice. But one of them happened to glance over his shoulder. He let out a cry, and the other looked too. By that time, of course, it was too late. I could do nothing about it."

"I guess not."

"They both yelled then," admitted George sadly, "and got into this thing you said is a car. It must have been frightened also, for it began to cry out in a terrible voice. Worse than that of Tyrannosaurus."

"Just the engine," interrupted Joey. "The car isn't alive."

"It moves," argued the stegosaurus. "It must be alive."

"So does a rock move when it rolls. So does a log when it floats in water. But they aren't alive."

"True," agreed George, but with reservation in his voice. "At the time I thought it was alive. It opened its closed eyes, and they glowed with fire. The dreadful voice continued to shriek, and the three of them started uproad. It was then that I remembered my promise to you."

"To follow if they went away?"

"Exactly. I wasn't nearly so shy as I imagined I would be. You see, the thieves and I had met — that is, we had seen each other, although we had never been introduced or had spoken. I feel that once you're over the first hurdle it isn't so bad. There's no need to be *quite* so shy."

"So you went after them?"

"I went after them." George nodded. "I called to them to stop, but this car-creature kept making such a noise that I'm sure they didn't hear me. One of the thieves looked back once, and I tried to motion, but they only went away all the faster. I do hope they didn't take your valuables with them."

"I'm afraid they did," said Joey sadly. "Unless they forgot and left it in the car."

"Why don't you look?" asked George sensibly.

Joey searched the car carefully, the glove compartment, both seats, the floor, every place he thought anyone might possibly hide money, but there was none to be found.

"I wonder why they left the car here anyway?" he said finally.

"That I don't know," said George. "They were gone when I arrived, since they could move faster than I could. But I remembered my promise. I followed until I came upon the car. It had stopped speaking then. And I did not see anything of the two thieves who were in it. It seemed best to wait here."

"I didn't meet them when I was coming out from Silo," said Joey. "Maybe they went back to the ranch."

"Not if they returned by road," argued George. "For I was on it every moment."

"Well, wherever they've gone," said Joey, trying to put down the disappointment of the thought of an alerted constable with no one to arrest, "I think I should take the professor's car back home. Besides, Daisy Belle ran away, and it's a long walk."

"Can you make it move?" asked George.

"I never have driven a car," admitted Joey. "But I've watched plenty of other people do it. It looks simple enough."

"Would you like me to get in with you? If you're the slightest bit nervous, I might have a calming effect. I really don't know what fear is."

"You're afraid of strangers."

"That's shyness," said George sharply. "I've told you that before. It's not the same thing at all."

"Well, anyway, I don't think you'd better try to get in," said Joey. "It's a small car. I don't think there'd be room for you."

"Oh, I'd likely knock off the roof. But I don't think it would hurt me much. My shields are made of bone and haven't much feeling." Clearly the stegosaurus was anxious to take a ride.

"Let me see if I can get it started first," said Joey hastily. He wondered if George would feel too hurt if he just ran off and left him. He didn't want the professor's car to be wrecked.

But the car wouldn't start. He stepped on the starter

again and again, and nothing happened but a metallic brr. Then he remembered to look at the gas gauge. It was empty.

"Seems like the day for running out of gas," he said in disgust.

This, fortunately, was not so serious as the mishap to Mr. Jones' plane. The professor kept a ten-gallon can of extra gas for his car at the ranch house. He probably intended to pour some in the next morning. Joey had remembered it yesterday and offered some to Mr. Jones, but it was not the same kind of gas used by planes, and the pilot had declined the offer.

"What's the matter?" asked George. "Why doesn't it move?"

"It's out of gas."

"What is gas?"

"It's what cars run on. It's like — it's like food. If you didn't get enough food, you'd be too tired to move, wouldn't you?"

"Certainly," agreed George with understanding. "Shall we try it on a little sagebrush?"

"That wouldn't work. It has to have a special kind of food. We have some at the ranch."

"Then we'll have to get it there somehow, the poor, starving thing."

"But how?"

"You might try coaxing it. Talk to it. Promise it food when it arrives. That might spur it on."

"It wouldn't work. Cars can't understand."

"Ah, then they really aren't alive after all," decided George, nodding wisely. "They have so many qualities — a voice, eyes that shine in the dark, the ability to move — all of them things that live creatures have, that I wondered if you weren't spoofing me."

"Maybe you could push it!" cried Joey suddenly.

George hesitated.

"I'd rather pull it," he admitted finally. "If you don't mind. It is a long way, and I'd have to push with my head. The strain might be hard on my brain, and I'm very careful of what brain I have."

"That's fine," agreed Joey enthusiastically. "There are ropes in the back seat with the professor's stuff."

It was a hard job attaching the ropes to the stegosaurus. They decided, after much deliberation, that lines should be hooked around one of the triangular shields. The only ones Joey could reach grew out at an angle parallel to the ground, and the rope slipped off at the slightest tug. It was necessary that the line be attached to a top shield which extended skyward. But even when George bent down, Joey couldn't reach any of these. Finally he climbed onto the hood of the car and from there to the top. George folded his back legs in such a manner that the top shields were only a few feet out of Joey's grasp. By tossing and retossing he managed to throw the rope around one of them and tie the ends to the bumper.

"That's one thing I'm going to start practicing tomorrow," he said grimly.

"What's that?" asked George.

"I'm going to learn how to use a lasso. Here I've lived on a ranch practically all summer, and I haven't learned yet."

"I don't know what it is," said George, "but I don't believe I know how either. And I've lived here longer than you have."

Joey got into the professor's car and grasped the wheel tightly. Even though the automobile was to be towed, he didn't want to miss this experience in steering. George started ahead. The ropes which connected the front bumper to one of the stegosaurus' topmost shields pulled taut, and the car moved a few feet. Then George stopped and the car stopped too.

"What's the matter?" cried Joey in alarm. "Is it too heavy?"

"Oh, it isn't that," said George. "It's those fiery eyes looking into my back. I don't like to be stared at."

"I'll fix that." Joey switched off the lights.

"That's better," said George with satisfaction. "I don't mind being looked at if whoever does it keeps his eyes closed."

Again the stegosaurus started forward, pulling the professor's car after him. He made a half circle to turn around, and Joey held tightly to the wheel, steering the car. It was a gratifying sensation. He had always known he could drive a car if someone would only give him a chance.

They did not make as good time as Joey wished, for

whenever George saw a particularly tantalizing clump of sagebrush growing close to the road he stopped to eat it. The car, of course, stopped too, and Joey had to sit and wait until George was ready to go on. It was a little irritating, but he decided it was better to say nothing. It was kind of George to tow the car, and nighttime was the animal's favorite grazing period.

At length they reached the turnoff from the main highway to the private road leading to the ranch on Cricket Creek. It was almost morning by this time. The sky, which had been so dark, was turning gray, and the stars were no longer close, but seemed smaller, farther away, and appeared to have lost some of their glitter.

Joey reminded himself that when they began the steep descent into the gully he must remember to put his foot

on the brake as the professor always did. It would never do to have the rolling car break away and smash into George's spiked tail. At that very moment the stegosaurus stopped again.

"I can't go any farther," announced George. "You'll have to untie me."

"But George, we're nearly home."

"Don't argue," said the stegosaurus sharply. "Do as I say. I am in extreme danger."

Joey got out of the car. He untied the ropes from the bumper and pulled one end so that they slipped off the bony shield. He was very disappointed. He had wanted so much to return the professor's car safely to the side yard. He wanted to bring it in himself and not have to report that it was sitting on the road. Of course, it couldn't possibly make up for the loss of the money, but it would be an accomplishment he could remember for a long time.

"I don't see what you're so excited about," he told George reproachfully. "I wanted to have the car sitting there when everybody woke up."

"They are awake now," said George testily.

Joey went to the edge and looked over. Sure enough, lights were burning in the ranch house. He realized that it was about the time the professor arose every morning, for he always tried to eat his breakfast early and arrive at the rocks as soon as he could see. Mrs. Brown always got up early to get his breakfast.

Since they were awake, they might have discovered that Mr. Jones and Mr. Smith were no longer in the barn. Perhaps someone had thought to look in the cookie jar and found that the money was no longer there. Certainly the professor had missed his car by now. Joey pictured their alarm, their sense of loss and helplessness. He decided that only one thing might take their minds from their worries, the same thing which had helped Joey to forget his. They must see him come driving in with the professor's stolen car.

"George," he said earnestly. "I've got to drive the car down the hill, and you'll just have to help."

"I can't," said George. "It's just too much to ask of friendship. I shouldn't even be here now. I must go back to my cave."

"There's still time. Everybody's in the house."

"I will not pull you down that road," said George, stamping one big padded foot petulantly.

"You don't have to. Just give me a push. A little tiny push. Then I'll be on the slope, and I can coast down by myself."

"Consider my brain, please," said George sulkily.

"You don't have to push with your head. Can't you stand sideways and sort of give me a shove? Then you can be off to your cave, and I'll promise never to ask another favor."

"Well — " George hesitated, but he finally gave in. "I'll try. But if it doesn't work, you'll just have to walk down and carry back some of the creature's food. You said yourself that as soon as it ate, it would be strong enough to move again."

Joey got back in the car and gripped the wheel tightly. George walked around behind and turned sideways. Joey heard him give a little grunt, and the car inched forward. George grunted again, and the car moved another foot. The front wheels were right on the edge of the sloping road now. Joey jiggled back and forth in an effort to help George move the car.

Suddenly he felt it start to roll. It went slowly at first, then gathered speed and went faster and faster. He clung to the wheel, trying to make the turns in the road, and the car went bumping and racing on, as though it had suddenly become alive. The car was almost at the bottom before Joey remembered that the professor always used the brake when going down this abrupt slope. He pressed his foot down hard on the pedal, but the car seemed to ignore the effort. He thought it was actually going even faster as they reached the level and shot across the yard.

He saw the canvas of the professor's tent rising to meet the car, and tried to turn the wheel to avoid it, still pushing on the brake as hard as he could. Apparently he hadn't started the turn in time, for the car came to an abrupt and noisy stop against a tent pole. Fearfully Joey looked around him. He had landed up in the very center of the professor's tent.

Chapter Eleven

Joey Brown, I am ashamed of you," cried his mother. "Taking the professor's car without asking. Why, you might have been killed. And just look what you've done to his tent!"

Mrs. Brown, Professor Harris, and Joan had rushed outside when they heard the squealing brakes and the rattle of overturned equipment as the car came to a stop against a tent pole. Joan had been awakened by the noise and was still in her pajamas.

"I didn't take it," said Joey in an injured tone. "I rescued it from the thief."

"What thief?" asked the professor.

"Mr. Jones."

"Mr. Jones isn't a thief," reproved Mrs. Brown. "Wherever do you get such wild ideas? And don't try to change the subject. We're talking about your taking the professor's car as you did."

"He is too a thief," contradicted Joey. "He took the money out of the cookie jar. I told you you should have hidden it someplace else."

Mrs. Brown looked a little embarrassed.

"I did," she confessed. "I knew it was silly to let you upset me, Joey, but I was a little worried. It's such a lot of money not to have in the bank. I took it to bed with me and hid it under my mattress. So now you ought to apologize to poor Mr. Jones for calling him a thief, although I guess it's better that he doesn't know you thought he was one."

"You mean you've got the money?" cried Joey. "It's safe, after all? Oh, my! When Mr. Jaeggers stops them at the bus, and shows his constable badge, and starts asking questions, it's going to be awfully embarrassing."

"What do you mean, Joey?" asked Professor Harris.

"Why, just that when I saw the cookie jar was empty I thought Mr. Jones had taken the money. So I rode into town and told Mr. Jaeggers. He thought Mr. Jones sounded like a crook too. So he's going to arrest him before he gets on the bus."

"I think I can take care of that," said Professor Harris. "I'll be there too, you know. I promised to drive them in. I can explain everything."

"But they've already gone," insisted Joey. "They were the ones who took your car. Anyway, they started to, but it ran out of gas and they left it sitting in the road. That's where I found it. I don't know where they went after that."

"How did you get into town?" asked Joan curiously.

"On Daisy Belle."

He looked quickly toward the barnyard. The old horse

had returned home and was standing patiently beside the fence.

"Joey, this is the wildest story yet," said Mrs. Brown, shaking her head.

"Suppose I walk over and see if our visitors, like Daisy Belle, have returned to the barn," said the professor. Joey had the feeling that the professor was trying hard not to smile. "You know, Joey, if they abandoned the car because they ran out of gas, it doesn't explain how you drove it back on an empty tank. You may have a little trouble figuring out an answer to that one."

Joey opened his mouth to tell them of George's help in towing the car, then closed it tightly. He remembered in time that he couldn't mention the stegosaurus. But how could he explain the return trip without doing so?

The professor crossed the yard and entered the barn lot. They heard him call, then he opened the doors and disappeared inside.

"He won't find them. They aren't there," said Joey positively.

Mrs. Brown looked at him reproachfully.

"You sure made a mess of the professor's tent," said Joan frankly.

"I'd like to see you do any better," retorted Joey in anger. "It's no cinch holding a car on that downhill. You try it, and you'll think I did pretty good."

"There'll be no more of that," said Mrs. Brown. "After this, no one touches the professor's car but the professor."

After a while Professor Harris returned. His face was puzzled.

"They're not there," he reported. "No signs of them either. They took everything they had."

"They didn't have anything but Mr. Smith's brief case," remembered Joan. "They left their bags in the plane and didn't think of them till it was time to go to bed and Mr. Smith wanted his toothbrush. Remember?"

"I remember," the professor agreed thoughtfully. "I can't understand why they stole away like this. I thought they agreed to take the morning bus. We would have plenty of time to make it."

"It wasn't very gentlemanly of them to take your car without asking," said Mrs. Brown. "It really served them right to run out of gas."

"How did you get it started, Joey?" demanded Joan. "If they couldn't make it run, how could you?"

Joey gave his sister a disgusted look. She, of all people, should know better than to ask questions. At that moment a possible solution came to her, and she clapped her hand over her mouth, looking a little ashamed of herself.

"Yes, how did you?" asked Mrs. Brown.

"Perhaps there was a little reserve in the tank, and after the engine cooled he was able to get it started," said the professor in a slightly befuddled voice. "To tell you the truth, I don't know anything at all about the mechanics of an automobile. But perhaps something

134

like that could occur. Thank you, Joey, for returning my car."

"You should have left it there," insisted Mrs. Brown. "A car is a powerful, dangerous thing."

"I wasn't in any danger, Mom," Joey assured her earnestly. "And the only scary part was right at the end, coming down that hill."

Mrs. Brown suddenly remembered the breakfast cooking away on the stove, and hurried inside. The professor and the children followed more slowly.

"I'm sorry about your tent," apologized Joey. "I'll clean everything up today."

"That's all right," smiled the professor. "Not much damage done except a few poles knocked loose. And I'll be taking them up in a day or so anyway."

The twins looked at each other with troubled eyes. The week was almost gone. Only today and tomorrow remained, then the professor would take down his tent, bundle his equipment into his car, and ride away from Cricket Creek. Soon after that they themselves would pack up and move back to town, in time for the opening of school, Mrs. Brown had said. They just couldn't live on their savings, and there was nothing else to do.

"Today," Joey told Joan, "we have to find a fossil. We just have to."

Mrs. Brown, however, had other ideas. Now that they believed Joey's story of his wild night's adventure, she made him repeat it in all detail.

135

"That's just too much excitement for one small boy," she declared when he had finished. "You haven't been asleep all night."

"I don't mind," said Joey. "It was fun."

"Fun or not," said Mrs. Brown, "you'll go to bed right after breakfast. You can't stay up all day and all night too."

"Mom, I can't," he protested.

"Oh, no," cried Joan. "We've got to hunt fossils. It's practically our last chance. You wouldn't do that to us, Mom?"

"I not only would, but I will," said Mrs. Brown firmly. "Joey is not going fossil hunting today. He's going to bed and sleep. When he wakes up, he's to straighten up the professor's tent, set everything to rights, and drive those stakes back in the ground."

"How about Joan?" said Joey. "Does she get to go fossil hunting?"

"I don't think she should. I don't like to have one of you off on the rocks alone."

"She could go with me." The professor hesitated. "But of course, I stay all day."

"I'd rather go to the rocks just above the ledge. The ones closest to home," insisted Joan. "We've never looked there. And I won't stay long. Nothing will happen, Mom. I'll be very careful. And we do have to leave here pretty soon."

Mrs. Brown finally agreed, and when the dishes were washed and dried Joan set off alone. She did not take Daisy Belle today. The old horse had had a hard trip the night before and deserved a rest. In spite of her brave words Joan was a little frightened at being out alone. Of course, there was nothing to be afraid of, unless she encountered a rattlesnake. But she had always had Joey along before.

Since she was not going to their usual meeting place, she couldn't even expect to see George. It would be nice to see him, she thought, and comforting to hear his voice in all this silence, but it meant a longer walk, and she had promised to stay close to home. She climbed the hill and turned immediately to the left, making her way to the beginning of the rimrock cliffs, where they dropped precipitously into the little valley which held the ranch buildings.

After she left the road the ground was rough and dusty, but when she reached the beginning of the rocks she saw that it was cut up even more. There were great holes in the earth, and mounds of dirt surrounding the holes. Against the bottom of the cliff she saw something white and went over to pick it up. It was heavy, despite its small girth and short length, and she realized she was holding stone.

A fossil! She had found a fossil! She had just walked over here, and there it was — lying out in plain sight. Pieces of the rock cliff had been broken off and lay crumbling about it.

"Oh!" she cried, forgetting there was no one there to hear her. "I've found one! I've found one!"

"What have you found, my little friend?" asked George. He materialized suddenly from the rocks and came toward her on his large silent feet.

"A fossil," she answered eagerly, too excited at her discovery to be surprised at his sudden appearance. "It's a bone! A dinosaur bone. I found it right here beside the rocks!"

The huge tail stopped wagging, and the armored plates bristled warningly. George took a few steps nearer, his bright eyes peering at the object in her hand. Then he stopped, and the tail again took up its side-to-side motion.

"Oh no, little friend," he said. "That didn't belong to one of my family. It didn't at all. That's just a mammal bone."

"Oh," said Joan in disappointment.

She remembered what the professor had said about a bone buried by a dog turning into a fossil after only a few hundred years, providing there was sufficient mineral in the soil. She hadn't found anything remarkable after all. Nothing important enough to cause the professor to remain at the ranch and continue his necessary board money. She glared at the chalk-white bone as though it were in some way to blame for not being other than it was. It was not more than six or seven inches long and broken off at one end. On the opposite end there were three separated lumps which might have once been toes. Obviously this was the leg bone of some small animal. George was right. It couldn't be a dinosaur.

"Do you know what kind of an animal it belonged to, George?" she asked without much interest.

George inspected the fossil specimen with distaste, then shook his head.

"No one important," he told her carelessly. "Just a mammal. A small one. It looks to me as though it might have belonged to a horse. I should think it might have been the leg, don't you?"

"It couldn't be a horse. It's too small for one. Why, even colts have longer legs than this."

"No doubt you're right," said George cheerfully. "You shouldn't ask me such questions. You know my brain is too small for the right answers."

"It's probably a coyote," decided Joan, and tossed it on the ground. There was no use taking it home. The professor wouldn't care about the fossilized bone of a coyote. That wouldn't prove his theory that dinosaur bones were to be found in this part of the country. But it was hard to give up so easily.

"You haven't noticed any other fossil bones down here, have you?"

"No," said George positively. "That's the only one. I dislodged that this morning when I was sharpening my tail. I don't know if Joey told you, but I had a very disturbing night."

"He told me." She nodded. There had been a few minutes before Mrs. Brown sent Joey to bed during which he had whispered a hurried account of the part George had played in the rescue of the car.

"I was very upset," confessed the stegosaurus. "All those strangers! And then, when Joey asked me to take another chance and pull the car down to your cave, I seemed to go all to pieces. I gave him a push, then I hurried over here. I couldn't wait to get to the hidden river. I just had to sharpen my tail immediately. I don't know when I've ever done such a thing before."

"I don't think it matters," Joan told him. "Pretty soon everybody is going away from here anyway."

"Not you?" cried George in alarm.

"Me. And Joey too. Everybody. Then you'll have this place all to yourself."

"But you can't do that," protested George. "I was so lonely before you came. I'll be lonely again. Why do you have to go away?"

"We can't support ourselves on the ranch. Things won't grow without water. All we have is the well, and we can't carry enough to keep the ground wet."

"You ought to eat sagebrush," advised George. "I find it very tasty myself. But how have you been living if you haven't had food?"

"We have food. We've been buying it with money."

"Money again!" exclaimed George in exasperation. "I just wish I had the brains to understand about money. Where do you get it?"

"We've had a boarder. The money he gives my mother for his meals and for his washing and ironing pays for our food. We haven't had to get into our savings. But now he's going away, so there won't be any more

board money, and we'll have to leave too."

"It seems very simple to me," declared George. "It doesn't take much brains to figure that out. You just keep him here. Then you won't have to leave either."

"He has to go. He hasn't found what he's looking for here."

"What is he looking for?"

"Fossils. Dinosaur tracks or bones."

The armored shields on the stegosaurus' back twitched with disapproval. He stalked up and down for a moment, too angry to speak. Suddenly he stopped, and the spiked tail whacked angrily against the ground. Dirt flew, and another bit of the cliff crumbled, disclosing a dull white splotch against the gray-brown rock.

"What's that?" cried Joan eagerly.

"Oh, just more of this mammal," said George carelessly. "I knocked loose the leg bone earlier when I sharpened my tail. There's more of the horse, or whatever it is, still left."

"Oh," said Joan in disappointment. "Then I guess there's no use in digging it out."

"Not unless you think it might be possible to fool the man who gives you money," said George slyly. "That might be worth a try. Tell him this is dinosaur bone. He'll never know the difference."

"We couldn't fool the professor. He's very smart. He'll know the difference in a minute."

"I don't see how he can tell, since he isn't a dinosaur himself," insisted George. "I have instinct to tell me this is a bone from a mammal. He wouldn't have that instinct."

"Oh, George," protested Joan. "This is a little bone. Dinosaurs had big ones."

"Not little dinosaurs," said George firmly. "There were all sizes, you know. Little ones and big ones. The more I think about it, the better I like the idea. It would be such a joke — and serve him right, too. Anyone who is mean enough to dig around for dinosaur bones deserves to have such a joke played on him. Let's do it. It's very funny."

"I don't think it is," insisted Joan. "Besides, it won't work."

"Extremely funny," insisted George. "I can hardly keep from laughing just to think of it. Why, it's the funniest thing I ever heard of. Imagine him digging and digging, thinking he's discovered a rare dinosaur bone, when all the time it's just another mammal. And, of course, all the while he'll be giving you more of that money you want. You've got to do it, Joan. You've simply got to."

"What do you want me to do?" she demanded, puzzled.

"Why, take him this bone, of course," explained George. "Tell him you found it here and that there's more in the rocks. I'd help you dig them out, but that would spoil the whole thing. I could do it in a few minutes. It will take him a long time, and the longer it takes, the more of that stuff called money you'll get."

"It won't work," declared Joan, shaking her head. "He'll know the difference in a minute."

"It won't hurt to try," insisted George. "Promise me you'll do it. Promise you'll tell him exactly what I told you to say. Bring him here. Show him the side of that cliff."

"But how about you? You don't want strangers hanging around your rocks."

"I can keep out of sight," said George. "He'll be busy here, and I'll know where he is, and stay around that stretch close to my hidden river. It's a nuisance, I'll admit, but you're my friends. I must do something to help you. Besides, it's such a joke."

He seemed to have his heart set on her presenting the fossilized bone to the professor, so Joan agreed. Nothing would come of it, she knew. Professor Harris had been only mildly interested when they returned with the plant fossil. He had smiled and told them it would be a nice start for a collection. Now they would have an addition to that collection, the petrified leg bone of something that looked suspiciously like a fox, or more probably a small coyote.

She hadn't much heart for today's search, but she knew she must do her best. Joey was depending on her. She poked about the cliffs, turning over loose rocks and studying them carefully for an impression of something which had no place being there. George did not bother to hunt today. He padded around, chuckles bubbling from his beaklike mouth every time he thought of the joke he had conceived against the professor. He could hardly wait to hear the results, so certain was he of success.

At last Joan looked at the sun and decided it was time to go home. The early hours of the morning were gone, and she was beginning to feel the heat. Mrs. Brown would begin to worry.

"Take the bone," George reminded her, "the bone from the horrid little mammal, and be sure you give it to the man at once. Tell him there's more where that came from."

"I will," promised Joan sadly. Poor George! There were times when she had considered him quite bright, at least of average intelligence. At the moment, however, she was convinced that everything people said about his little brain was true. This bone wouldn't fool the professor for one minute.

It was really hot by the time she reached the ranch on Cricket Creek, and Mrs. Brown had all the doors closed and the blinds pulled down at the windows. Joan walked into the kitchen and tossed the fossilized bone on the table. It landed with a heavy thud.

"What's that?" asked Mrs. Brown curiously.

"A fossil I found. It's the bone of some animal. A coyote probably."

"Then get it off the table. That's where we eat, Joan. I don't want a dirty old bone where we're going to put clean food later on."

Joan picked up the fossil and looked for a place to put

it. She didn't see a likely spot, so she dropped it on the floor back of the door.

"Where's Joey?" she asked. "Did he go to sleep?"

"Of course." Mrs. Brown nodded. "He didn't want to, but he was worn out and couldn't keep awake. We'd better keep quiet. He needs his rest."

"All right," agreed Joan listlessly. She sat down in one of the rockers and began rocking violently. It was the one that squeaked, and a chorus of little protests, like the alarmed voices of a colony of mice, filled the room.

"Joan," reproved Mrs. Brown quickly. "I asked you to be quiet."

"Yes, Mom."

She stopped rocking and sat still. Mrs. Brown was sewing, and the only sound was the ticking of the metal alarm clock on the window sill. It was an irritating sound to Joan. Tick, tick, tick, tick, as fast as it could go, as though it were running a race. So it was, she told herself. It was time racing against her and Joey. If time won, they would have to go back to town. Joan wanted to get away from the sound.

"I'm going out to the barn," she announced, standing up.

"What for?" asked Mrs. Brown mildly. "What is there to do out there? You won't have Joey to play with."

"I don't want to play," said Joan. "I want to think."

Mrs. Brown made no objection, and Joan went outside into the pressing heat of a sun nearing midday. There was a little breeze, but it only stirred the heat around more fiercely, blowing it against her face like the air from a baking oven when the door is first opened. The vegetables were beginning to droop again, she noticed. Try as they would, she and Joey couldn't carry enough buckets of water to keep the soil around the plants moist. It took more than a few containers splashed on twice a day. In this climate crops needed regular and scientific irrigation. The one hen left after the coyote raid scuttled along before her, picking at bugs. The hen didn't seem to mind the heat. If they only had a coyote-proof hen house, they could probably raise chickens. But that, like everything else, took money, and there just wasn't enough.

Joan pushed open the barn door and walked inside. It was shadowy, and after coming directly from sunlight it gave the first impression of coolness. It wasn't really cool after the first few minutes, but she didn't mind that. It smelled of hay and dust and old leather.

She went over to one of two overturned wooden boxes and sat down. She and Joey used the boxes for seats when they played checkers and old maid and some of the other games they had brought from town. It was funny, but the games which had seemed old and tiresome before took on a new freshness when they were played in the barn.

Today, however, Joan was in no mood for playing games, even if she had had someone to play with. She sat on the box and stared disconsolately at the wall. Light came through some of the cracks, like long inserts of sparkling glitter against the rough, dark wood. As she watched, the hot wind caught at the open doors, and one of them creaked slowly shut. They needed new hinges badly.

For several moments she stared at the door without knowing what was different. She had looked at it a hundred times, and in a way it seemed the same today. But there was a slight difference. Something green, a leaf probably, was stuck to one of the boards. That was strange, she decided. The only green leaves around here were in the small garden plot close to the house. How could a leaf travel so far and stick to the inside of the barn door afterward?

Curiosity finally made her get to her feet and cross the floor to investigate. The leaf, or whatever it was, was stuck on a nail a little above her eye level. She reached up to take it down, and discovered it was a piece of green paper. Then she began to scream with excitement. She rushed out of the barn and across the barn lot with the green paper still in her hands. She didn't mean to lose that. It was a hundred-dollar bill!

Chapter Twelve

JOAN RUSHED into the kitchen carrying her discovery.

"Look!" she screamed. "Look what I found in the barn!"

"Sh!" said Mrs. Brown. "I warned you to be quiet."

"But it's a hundred dollars. A hundred-dollar bill!"

"What?" It was Mrs. Brown's turn to forget the need for silence. "Joan! You must be mistaken. Let me see it."

Joan gave it to her mother, who turned it over and over in her hands.

"See if it's like the others in the cookie jar," advised Joan. "Maybe it isn't a real one."

"It's real all right," said Mrs. Brown in a wondering tone. "Where did you find it?"

"On a nail. In the barn door."

"Hey! What's going on? What's happening?" Joey appeared in the doorway, rubbing puffy eyes.

"Look!" cried Joan. "A hundred-dollar bill. I just found it in the barn."

"Where?" Joey was wide awake now.

"Hanging on a nail in the door."

"It wasn't there yesterday."

"I know it wasn't. But it was there today."

"It must have been Mr. Smith," decided Mrs. Brown. "But why would he leave a hundred dollars?"

"Maybe it was rent for sleeping in the barn," suggested Joan. "He thought five dollars wasn't too much for lunch. Maybe he thought the barn was worth a hundred."

"Nonsense," said Mrs. Brown firmly.

"Maybe it wasn't Mr. Smith at all," said Joey. "Maybe it was your Uncle Henry's ghost. The one who left you this ranch when he died. Maybe he came back and left the bill there for a clue to tell us he'd hidden a lot more money in the barn — and all we have to do is find it."

"Oh, Joey!" said Mrs. Brown. "There aren't such things as ghosts, and even if there were, Uncle Henry didn't have any money. He only had this ranch, and he hadn't even paid the taxes on that for the last two years."

"He could have been a miser, and didn't want people to know he had money," insisted Joey stubbornly. Suddenly he was struck with a new idea. He turned his back so his mother couldn't see as he silently mouthed the words to Joan. "Maybe it was George."

"It couldn't be," she answered. "You were with him last night and I was this morning. He didn't have time. Besides, he doesn't understand about money."

"You and Joey were with whom?" asked Mrs.

Brown sharply. "With Uncle Henry? Joan, what are you talking about?"

"Nothing," said Joan quickly. "Just talking to myself. I was thinking about something else, and I guess I just thought aloud."

"Oh," said Mrs. Brown, mollified. "Well, it just has to be Mr. Smith's money. And we don't know his address or even his first name, so how can we return it to him?"

"We can't," Joan told her happily. "We might as well put it in the cookie jar with the rest."

"Just to be sure, we'd better search the barn," insisted Joey. "We'll look on all the nails and under all the boxes and hay. There just might be more."

It was obviously impossible for Joey to go back to sleep, so Mrs. Brown said he might dress. She wouldn't let him search for hidden money in the barn, however, until he had repaired the damage to the professor's tent. Joan helped him, and by the time they had finished, lunch was ready. After that there were dishes, and the afternoon had well begun before they got to the barn.

"I don't think there is any more, anyway," said Joan. "We're just wasting our time."

"Can you think of anything better to do with it?" demanded Joey. "How'd you do this morning?"

"Oh, I found a fossil bone, but it's not a dinosaur. It looks more like a coyote. A little one at that. George says it's a mammal, and he made me bring it home to fool the professor."

"You can't fool the professor," said Joey sagely. "He

151

may not know much about cars. Imagine him thinking there was reserve gas somewhere and that's how I got home! But he sure knows his fossils."

They worked diligently, and Joey would not rest until they had gone over every wall, dug in each corner, pried up boards that seemed to be loose, and turned over the hay. There were no more hundred-dollar bills. Joan had found the only one.

"I guess it must have been Mr. Smith's," she decided.

"But why'd he leave it? So much, I mean?"

"There's probably a very sensible reason if we could only think of it," said Joey.

The professor returned about dusk, and the children met him beside the newly repaired tent.

"Any luck?" called Joey.

"Not a thing," said the professor. "Same as ever. I'm going to give up this section. No sense in looking for a needle in a haystack, and that's about what it is. I'm still sure they're here, but I can't dig up the whole mountain to find them. I've got to go on some place where the indications are more evident."

"There's still one more day," reminded Joan.

"I'll spend it getting packed up and rested," said the professor. "Then I'll get an early start the next morning."

He went to his tent to get cleaned up, and the children wandered disconsolately into the kitchen.

"He's through looking," Joan told her mother. "Tomorrow he's going to pack, and the next day he's going on."

"You can't blame him," said Mrs. Brown. "It seems to me that it's a discouraging way to make a living. Did you tell him about the hundred-dollar bill?"

They had forgotten, but the moment the professor appeared, wearing a clean shirt, his hands and face freshly scrubbed, and his hair combed, they proceeded to do so. He listened with astonishment but could offer no better reason for the bill than they could.

"It's too much for a night's lodging," he decided. "At least for lodgings in a barn."

As Mrs. Brown finished placing the last dish on the table, the back door slammed shut with a violent bang. It and the windows had been opened at sundown, and a breeze blowing through had made a draft.

"You'll have to prop it open with something, Joey," said Mrs. Brown. "That's turning into a real wind out there. I wonder if we're going to have another thunderstorm."

Joey opened the door and looked around for something to use as a prop.

"This will do," he decided, bending over. "It's that fossil bone you found today, Joan. I guess it's of some use after all. It'll make a good doorstop."

"Fossil?" said Professor Harris. He had just started to pull out a chair, but now he left it and walked over to where Joey was standing. "Let me see it, Joey."

Joey gave it to him and made a prop of his own body to keep the wind from blowing back the door. His mother was right, he decided, the breeze was turning into a real wind. It was still warm, but the rush of air had lost some of its fire. If it weren't growing so dark, it would have been fun to fly a kite.

At the table Mrs. Brown waited politely for the professor to finish looking at the fossil. It seemed to take a long time, and he kept turning it over and over in his hands.

"It isn't a dinosaur, is it?" asked Joan.

"No," said the professor absently. "Not reptile. Not dinosaur."

"It is a mammal, isn't it?"

He looked up, as though someone had called to him from a great distance. His face wore a curious expression.

"Did you find this, Joan?" he asked sharply. "Did you find it today?"

"Yes."

"Where?"

"At the very beginning of the cliffs. Just up from the house. There's more, too, but I didn't bother to bring them home. I couldn't anyway. They're stuck in the rocks. You're sure it isn't a dinosaur? There were little ones, too, as well as big ones."

"It's a mammal," agreed the professor. "I'll have to get another opinion, of course. I can't be sure. But I think — I'm almost certain — that this is a real discovery."

"But you said it wasn't a dinosaur," cried Joey in surprise.

"It isn't. But, if it's what I think it is, it was here at the time of the dinosaurs. I think this is the leg bone of the four-toed horse. Of Eohippus, the dawn horse. And if it is, he was alive fifty million years ago."

"Jeepers!" cried Joey in excitement. "Then it's bound to be pretty valuable, isn't it? How much is it worth?"

Chapter Thirteen

THE NEXT MORNING Joan took Professor Harris to the face of the cliff where George's lashing tail had exposed another glimpse of white bone. The children had been a little amazed at the extra supplies he put in the back seat of the old car, some of which didn't seem quite right for such an expedition. Besides the usual chisels, shovels, and brushes, he took a roll of burlap, a can of varnish, and, most incredible of all, a sack of flour.

"Are you going to cook?" asked Joan politely.

"No," said the professor, smiling. "But I want to be prepared for any emergency."

George was nowhere to be seen when they arrived, otherwise the place looked just as it had the day before.

"I wonder what made these holes in the ground," said the professor absently, but he really wasn't concerned with them. He was too busy studying the white splotches of bone in the cliff. "It looks as though someone had been digging here."

"I wonder who," said Joey, grinning knowingly at his sister.

The professor went immediately to the face of the cliff, and his red face glowed with enthusiasm and pleasure.

"Yes, yes," he said to himself. "It must be. It has to be. At last!"

He brought his chisels and brushes from the car and went to work with the latter, whisking away dirt and loose sediment. The white seemed to grow even whiter, but there were still dark stripes of rock between the light patches.

"I do believe it's a rib section!" cried the professor. "I'll have to be very careful removing this. It will take much time and a lot of patience."

"You mean you'll be here the rest of the summer?" cried Joey.

"Yes indeed." The professor nodded. He picked up one of the steel chisels and began chipping away at the rock surrounding one of the narrow white stripes. "I'll work until the weather stops me late in the fall. Perhaps I can get a leave of absence. With a find like this, I'm sure the school will be sympathetic. I do want to get it out before winter, so perhaps I'll have to bring in help. Bigelow, maybe. He'll come at the drop of a hat when he hears about this."

The twins looked at each other in ecstasy. Two boarders! Double the money which was put in the cookie jar each week, plus whatever the museum would pay for the fossils. Surely their mother wouldn't insist on them returning to town now!

"You shouldn't work too long today, Professor," Joey reminded him. "You know you want to get that leg shipped in to the museum people. We won't know how much it's worth till they look at it."

"I know," agreed the professor. "But I can't leave this now. It's too fascinating. I'd like to get one rib exposed at least. We can go back to the house around noon if it looks as though it will take longer. That will give me plenty of time to drive into Silo and get the leg on its way."

"I can't get over this bone being a horse," said Joan. She spoke loudly, just in case George might be lurking nearby within earshot. Yesterday he had been a little embarrassed that he had suggested such a thing, and she wanted him to know he was right after all.

"Oh, Eohippus didn't look much like the horses of today," said the professor cheerfully. "He was no bigger than a fox. He had no mane, only a few stiff hairs on his neck, and a small tail, not a long, flowing one. He had four toes on each of his front feet and three toes on each back one. That was a back leg you found yesterday, Joan. The toes were what gave me the clue to his identity. Of course, it could be Mesohippus, but I don't think so. The leg bone is too short."

"Who's Mesohippus?" demanded Joey darkly.

"He's the in-between horse," said the professor. "He had three toes on each foot, and the middle one was biggest. Eventually it turned into a hoof. But Mesohippus himself was larger, as large as a big dog. Besides, the toes on this specimen seem to be of uniform size, so I think our first guess is right."

"Even if it is Mesohippus, it still ought to be worth something," decided Joey.

"Imagine little four-toed horses running around here," said Joan. "There must have been grass here then for them to eat."

"Oh, they didn't eat grass," objected the professor. "Their teeth weren't made for eating grass. Besides, there was none for them to eat at that time. This was a swampy country with just the beginning of woods at the time of Eohippus. He ate leaves from bushes."

Joan looked out onto the rough, dry, rolling plain. She couldn't imagine it covered with swamps and trees and green bushes. It seemed to her that it must always have been this way, arid and brown, lined with rimrock cliffs, and growing nothing but sagebrush and occasional clumps of tough, wiry grass. But it must have been different at one time. The professor said so.

"Then the swamps dried up," continued the professor, warming to his lecture, his fingers working busily all the while. "The trees spread, and the ground grew firmer. That's when Mesohippus made his appearance. Then the climate got even drier, and the woods disappeared. Grass came, and Mesohippus began to change too. The first change was his teeth. They had to change, you see, because now he had to eat grass. Low-branching trees and shrubs were hard to find. He grew taller; his neck grew longer. He ran swiftly now, because he couldn't take cover in the forests from his enemies, and he ran on one toe, the middle one. And then he wasn't Mesohippus any more. He was Protohippus, the 'just-before' horse."

"Do you think you might find some of their bones around here too?" asked Joey calculatingly.

"We might," agreed the professor. "There's no telling what we'll find. That's what makes this job so interesting. All we need is an indication, a hint on where to begin the search. You gave that to me, Joan."

"I'm glad." She beamed. "And I'm glad you're going to stay the rest of the summer too."

"Of course I am," said the professor. He seemed surprised that she could have even thought he might do anything else. "Not only this summer, Joan, but probably many summers to come. And don't think I'll be the only one."

"You won't?" cried Joey in amazement. "You mean that other people will come here to hunt fossils?"

"I'm sure of it. When news of this discovery gets out, you'll have more fossil hunters around than you've ever seen before. A lot of them will be amateurs, people who think it's an enjoyable way to pass a Sunday afternoon. Some will be students, classes here on field trips. And there will be other scientists besides me. They won't just search in this place, either. They'll go up and down these rocks like a swarm of bees."

"Oh, boy!" cried Joey, his eyes shining.

Joan looked toward the cliffs above them, searching for something colored like one of the rocks that might move in a way no rock was ever known to do. She hoped

that George was near enough to hear, and that he understood what he had done for them. He had thought to
fool the professor into thinking the fossil of a mammal
was that of a dinosaur. The professor hadn't been fooled,
but the scheme had worked anyway. The mammal had
been an important discovery, and all the credit went to
George. If he hadn't urged her, she wouldn't even have
bothered to carry it home. With regular boarders every
summer, surely they could manage for themselves during the winter months.

As the morning slipped by and the sun reached higher and higher in the sky, Joey reminded the professor again of his intention to get the leg bone on its way to the museum.

"I suppose we must go," agreed Professor Harris. "But it's hard to leave. I hate to tear myself away."

"You've got this rib sticking out pretty far," observed Joey. "I can get my finger in on both sides."

"The dangerous stage," agreed the professor. "I can't leave it like that, certainly."

He went to the car and returned with an armload of material which he placed on the ground. The children watched as he dipped a brush in the can of shellac, then carefully painted the exposed rib bone. He went over it again and again, and the dull white stripe glistened and sparkled in the sunlight. Then the professor left the shellacked bone, and in a workmanlike manner began mixing up a thick paste from flour and some of the water from his canteen.

"Hand me that burlap, Joey," he said, and when Joey had done so he cut off a narrow strip with his pocket-knife.

"I don't get it," puzzled Joey. "I don't get it at all."

"I'm making a bandage. This is the way fossils are prepared for shipping. Although they're stone, there's always a chance of their chipping or breaking off. This is just to make sure they won't do that."

"You think flour-and-water paste will do it?"

"It will when it dries. I'll soak the burlap in it, then lay it on the fossil. When it dries, it will form a hard shell, and when it finally arrives at the museum they can soak it off. The bone will be just as you see it now."

"But how will you get the rest of it out of the rock?"

"I'll have to chisel it out. This is an extra precaution in case my chisel slips."

They went back to the car, and the professor reloaded his equipment in the back seat. As he prepared to open the front door, however, he paused, took off his glasses, and polished them a moment before he put them back on.

"What's the matter, Professor?" asked Joan.

He was staring at the side of the cliff which they had left only a moment before, and his face was thoughtfully disturbed.

"I must be seeing things," he admitted. "Or maybe it was too much sun shining down on my head while I was working. I thought I saw a portion of that rocky wall move. Just above where we were standing, too."

"I don't see a thing," said Joey quickly. "It looks perfectly solid to me."

"I hope so," admitted the professor. "If it should suddenly crumble and slide right there and cover up our discovery, I don't think I could stand it."

"Oh, I'm sure it won't," Joan said soothingly. "Joey's right. It looks very solid. And there's hardly ever falling rocks unless it's wintertime and there's been bad weather."

"You're right, of course," agreed the professor. He got into the car and started the engine. "I was imagining things."

When they drove down the hill, they saw that a car was occupying the space beside the front door of the ranch house.

"Is it Mr. Blackwood?" asked Joan in amazement. "Maybe he stopped by on his way into town."

"That's not Mr. Blackwood's car," said Joey scornfully. "You sure don't know much about cars. His is a Chevrolet. This is a Ford."

"It's the same color," said Joan defensively.

"Sure. Black. There's probably a million cars painted black in the United States too."

"Then whose car is it?"

"The easiest way to find out," said the professor quickly, before Joey had a chance to answer, "is to go in the house and see who is there."

The twins piled out of the car and rushed toward the back door. Joey got his hand on the knob, but before he could open it Joan stopped him.

"Joey, do you think that was George the professor saw up on the rocks?"

"Sure. It couldn't have been anyone else."

"I'm glad he was there," said Joan. "I'm glad he heard the professor say he'd stay on the rest of the summer and even come back next year. George wanted to help us so much, and he really has, hasn't he?"

"I'll say," agreed Joey. "And another thing, we'd better not tell George the professor saw him. It'll only get him upset. He thinks he's really safe when he's standing against those rocks."

They heard Mrs. Brown's voice as they opened the door. She was talking with someone, and it must have been an exciting discussion, for her tone was high and sort of breathless with disbelief. They came in quickly, closing the door fast to keep out the heat. Sitting in one of the two rocking chairs was Mr. Jones.

Chapter Fourteen

H<small>I, KIDS</small>," said Mr. Jones.

They answered automatically, but Joey's eyes in particular were a little wary. It was hard to look at someone who for a long time he had been certain was a bad man, and then have to change his whole theory and admit he had been wrong. Besides, Joey was a little worried that Mr. Jones might ask about George. Mr. Jones and Mr. Smith had caught a glimpse of the stegosaurus the night they had left in such a hurry. Joey was never quite sure how his mother might react to some things. If he again insisted on knowing such a creature, she might take it in her head to bundle the whole family off to town, just as the future was brightening.

"Mr. Jones has been telling me about that hundred-dollar bill," said Mrs. Brown eagerly. "It wasn't what we thought at all. Mr. Smith left it for the professor."

"For the professor?" cried Joan. "I thought it was ours."

"It really belongs to the bank," said Mr. Jones. "I wouldn't be surprised if they'd want it back."

"And the five dollars he gave me for lunch too," said Mrs. Brown, nodding her head. "I'll return that right away."

"You won't lose anything," said Mr. Jones. "Thanks to your young hero here who smelled a thief."

He looked squarely at Joey as he spoke, and suddenly Joey's knees felt so weak that he had to sit down. The professor came in just then, and he and Mr. Jones greeted each other.

"Tell them the whole story," urged Mrs. Brown. "Just as you told me. I'd like to hear it again. I just can't believe that Mr. Smith is a bank robber. He seemed such a nice little man."

"Well, not a bank robber exactly," objected Mr. Jones. "What I mean is, he didn't walk in and pull a gun and hold it up. He was just a little mixed up in his mind, I guess. He'd worked there a long time, and some way or other — I still don't know exactly how — he concocted this plan to abscond with a good-sized roll. A hundred thousand dollars' worth, they said."

"Not Mr. Smith!" objected Joan. "Not the man who used to hunt sea shells when he was a little boy."

"You mean he had it with him? Here?" asked the professor.

"In his brief case. He was mighty careful of that brief case. Wouldn't let anybody else touch it or let it out of his sight. I noticed that right away, but I didn't think much about it until later."

"My, my! Think of that much money right here on our kitchen table!" marveled Mrs. Brown.

"Are you a private eye?" demanded Joey, suddenly recovering his voice. "Were you tailing him?"

"No," denied Mr. Jones cheerfully. "I'm just a pilot. A dumb one, too, or I'd have caught on sooner. You see, I've got a small outfit in Chicago. A couple of planes. We're picking up a little work here and there, just getting started. Well, one day this guy Smith—only that isn't his real name — came in to see me. He said he had to make a rush trip to the West Coast in a few days. He was a little vague on time. Said it depended on when he finished up his business in Chicago. He wanted to hire me to fly him out."

"Had you ever seen him before?" interrupted the professor.

"Never laid eyes on him. I explained that we usually didn't take passengers. Just light freight. And I asked him why he didn't get a seat on one of the regular passenger lines. He said it was because his plans were so uncertain and, once he was ready to go, he wanted to leave right then. He didn't know ahead of time exactly when that would be. Well, the fee he offered was a good one, and I didn't want to turn it down. I told him, sure, I'd take him, and he told me to be ready to take off on practically no notice. That's what he gave me too. No notice. He walked in at five o'clock a couple of days later and wanted to take off right then."

"Did you?" demanded Joey.

"Quick as I could," agreed Mr. Jones. "In about thirty minutes, I guess. Well, we took off, heading west for L.A., and we hadn't been in the air two hours before he began to talk about Mexico. Wanted to know if I could take him there instead, and would he have to have a passport to land. I told him he would, so he lost all interest in that. Instead, he began to think about going to San Francisco instead of L.A. I figured later on that maybe he got to thinking about the guys at the field. They knew where I was headed, and if someone had come around asking questions they would have told them. Anyway, I changed course and swung back north. I didn't put down where I'd intended to take on gas in the first place, so that's why we landed where we did."

"But he said he was going to Los Angeles," said Joey. "He said he had business there."

"He changed his mind again about an hour later," said Mr. Jones. "Then he changed it again. I bet I jigged and jagged a dozen times while he tried to make up his mind where he wanted to go. He was nervous and jumpy, and he had me going south, then north, then south again. After a while I got fed up and told him every time he changed his mind I was going to charge him a hundred bucks, but he didn't turn a hair. Money was no object to him."

"I should think not," said Mrs. Brown disapprovingly. "The money he was going to pay you with didn't belong to him."

"Finally we ran out of gas," continued Mr. Jones. "Smith was pretty upset at first, then it didn't seem to matter. He liked the idea of being here. And he seemed to like the idea of going on by bus. Any bus. No matter where it was headed."

"Then he didn't really have an appointment," said the professor.

"Not him," said Mr. Jones scornfully. "He was just on the lam, only he didn't know how to go about it. After we went to bed, he got to talking about that northbound bus. Thought he might even go into Canada. I asked him about his business, and he said it would keep. All he could think of was getting on that bus. But there was no way of getting into town except the professor's car, and Smith didn't want to wake him up. He said you folks had been nice enough to him already and he didn't want to bother you any more. He figured it would be easier to buy the car."

"Buy my car?" cried the professor in surprise. "It's not for sale. I've had it for several years, and I'm used to it. Of course, it's not the newest model, but I like it."

"He asked me how much it was worth," said Mrs. Jones, not looking at the professor, "and I told him not much. As you say, it's a pretty old model. I doubt if you'd get over fifty or seventy-five dollars for it. Smith decided to give you a hundred."

"And that was the money we found in the barn," said Mrs. Brown triumphantly.

"He offered me fifty bucks to drive him into town," continued Mr. Jones. "You see, he didn't know how to drive himself. By this time I figured he was a real crackpot, and decided to play along. He was so set on going that I knew he'd try to drive it himself if I didn't, and I knew he'd just leave the car in Silo. I figured I could tell somebody in town, and they could send word to the professor to come after his car. That way, he'd still have it and be a hundred bucks ahead."

"You should have guessed something was wrong right then," said Joey darkly.

"I guess I should," agreed Mr. Jones amiably. "Well, we sneaked out of the barn and over to the car. I'd just got in when Smith let out a screech that'd raise the dead. He yelled there was a monster after us and to get going."

"A monster!" repeated Mrs. Brown. "It was probably his own guilty conscience."

"Did you see a monster?" asked Joan in a quavering voice.

"I couldn't have," admitted Mr. Jones, frowning. "I thought I saw something, and later on in the road, when we ran out of gas, it seemed like something was coming after us. Now that I try to think what it looked like I couldn't tell you. Except that it was big and funny-shaped and sort of moved along without making any noise."

"Tumbleweed!" The professor laughed. "That's what you saw. A big clump of tumbleweed."

"Maybe so," grinned Mr. Jones. "But it sure raised the hairs on the back of my neck. After we left the car and saw it again, we started running up the road. We ran till we couldn't run any more, and we decided we'd have to sit down to rest. We went off the road apiece, and we were resting there when you came by, Joey. I'd just started to yell at you when Smith clapped his hand over my mouth. He said there was no time to stop and visit with anyone and we'd better let you go."

"I heard you," said Joey with satisfaction. "It was just like you said too. You started to call, then it stopped in the middle of a word."

"While we were sitting there resting," continued Mr. Jones, "I got to thinking about all the funny things Smith had done since I met him. Wanting to charter a private plane and leave on a minute's notice. Wanting to change course after he started. Not knowing which way he wanted to go. Throwing his money around like water. It just didn't add up, or else it added up too much. Then I got to thinking about Smith's brief case. It was the only luggage he had brought, and he sure was mighty careful of it. I wondered if it was really papers inside, the way he said."

"Paper money," said Joey triumphantly. He was feeling pretty good about things. True, he had picked the wrong man, but there had been thieves about.

"I tried to get him to let me carry it for him, but he hung on tighter than ever. By that time I was pretty sure there was something wrong. I decided I'd stick close to his coattails until I found somebody in authority. He could have had a gun."

"They always do," Joey nodded.

"When we got into Silo, the town was dark except for one house. There was a downstairs light on in the house next to the general store."

"Why, that's Mr Jaeggers' house," said Mrs. Brown.

"I decided to see if I could pull a fast one," confessed Mr. Jones with a little laugh. "I knew I ought to get to a

telephone. You can always get the police by calling central. So I started talking about how good a cup of hot coffee would taste. Of course, there wasn't any place open where you could buy one, but I pointed out this light. I told Smith we might be able to talk the lady of the house into making us a cup. He didn't think much of the idea, but I finally talked him into it. For anybody smart enough to get away with a roll like that in the first place, he was sure dumb about covering up his tracks. We went up to the door and knocked, and pretty soon an old geezer in a pair of pants, but no shirt or shoes, came to the door."

"That's Mr. Jaeggers," whispered Mrs. Brown to the professor. "You've seen him at the store."

"I told him our problem, that we were waiting for the northbound bus, expecting to flag it down when it went through, and we wondered if we could get him to make us a cup of coffee. He kind of hesitated and said he

wasn't running a short-order restaurant. Then he asked
us our names. When we told him, he seemed to change
his mind. He opened the door wider and told us to come
in and sit down. Then he went into the other room for a
minute. I looked around, trying to locate the telephone,
and the next thing I knew he was back and he had a
gun."

"What kind of a gun?" demanded Joey. "A revolver?"

"No," denied Mr. Jones. "A shotgun. A double-
barreled shotgun. I guess Mr. Jaeggers goes hunting in
the fall. Anyway, he stood there, waving the muzzle back

and forth from one to the other of us, and said, 'All right, where's the money you stole? Hand over the stolen money right now.'"

"Oh, my!" said Joan. "How did he know about it?"

"Ask your brother," grinned Mr. Jones.

"But that wasn't the money I meant," admitted Joey honestly. "I meant the money in our cookie jar. And I didn't suspect Mr. Smith. I thought it was —"

"I know," said Mr. Jones genially. "You thought it was me. I've been a lot of things in my life, kid, but not that. Anyway, you had the general idea, just the wrong guy. And it worked. Smith handed over his brief case, meek as a lamb, and he began to babble about how the bank drove him to it. It was their fault, he said. They worked him hard, with not much pay, and kept all that dough around to tempt him. It didn't take Jaeggers and me long to figure out the score then. We got on long-distance, and, sure enough, Mr. Smith was wanted. Bad."

"Just imagine such a thing!" said Mrs. Brown.

"Yes, imagine him thinking that I'd want to sell my car," fumed the professor. "And that I'd only ask a hundred dollars for it."

"I'd give you more than that for it," said Joey. "If I had it, that is."

"Better be careful what you say, young man." Mr. Jones laughed. "Because you will have it. When I was talking to Chicago, they said something about a reward. I may be wrong, but I think five thousand was the figure mentioned. Jaeggers and I decided it belongs to you."

Chapter Fifteen

THE NEXT FEW DAYS proved to be so filled with exciting things to do that the children had no time to go looking for George. There were two boarders at the ranch
on Cricket Creek now, for Mr. Jones persuaded Mrs.
Brown to cook for him also. He slept in the barn, and
after Joey and Joan explained that Daisy Belle was old
and accustomed to go inside at night, he obligingly left
the door open. He refused to ride a horse, Mr. Jones said,
but he didn't mind sharing his bedroom with one.

Mr. Jones had rented a car while he was there, and he
usually invited the twins to go with him. Every day they
drove into Silo to see if his ordered plane parts had arrived. Joey liked to go to Silo these days. Everyone
smiled at him approvingly, and he knew he was being
pointed out as the hero who had first recognized the
thief. They drove out to the place where the wrecked
plane was still sitting, and Mr. Jones removed the dam-
aged portions, getting everything ready for the installa-
tion of new ones.

One day when they were in Mr. Jaeggers' store Mr.

Jones purchased a sack of nails and a couple of new hinges.

"What are you going to do with those?" asked Joey curiously. "You don't use nails like that on airplanes."

"You do in barns and houses and fences," said Mr. Jones. "I've noticed a few loose boards around your ranch. You oughtn't to let things like that go, not with winter coming on. They just get worse and worse, and the first thing you know, you have to tear down and build over."

"Are you going to fix up the ranch for us?" asked Joan.

"I'd rather be doing that than sitting around," said Mr. Jones. "Some people can sit and do nothing. Our friend, Mr. Smith, for instance. But it gives me the jitters."

Joey flushed as he remembered that Mr. Jones' impatience at inactivity had been one of the things which made him suspect the pilot of being something other than he was.

"I'll help you," he said quickly. "We'll both help."

So the twins and Mr. Jones started making repairs about the place. They propped and reinforced sagging fences, put the new hinges on the barn door, renailed loose boards. They even climbed up on the roof and tacked down a few shingles which might have been ripped off by a winter gale.

"My goodness," said Mrs. Brown. "The way you three are fixing things up, you'd think we meant to stay here."

"Don't you?" said Mr. Jones in surprise.

"Why, no. I have to make a living."

"There's a living here, and a good one," objected Mr. Jones. "At least there will be as soon as the government finishes that new dam. This section of the country will be included in that new reclamation project."

"I don't understand," said Mrs. Brown, bewildered.

"Irrigation," explained Mr. Jones. "There's nothing wrong with the soil. It just needs water."

"But there isn't any water except in the well," said Joan.

"Those miles between here and the river will melt fast when the dam is finished. There'll be power then and irrigation ditches. You won't know this country in a few years. It will be rich and valuable."

"You mean I could make something by selling the ranch?" asked Mrs. Brown.

"Not now. Not till the dam's finished. Then you can. Prices will skyrocket when that happens."

"How long will it take?" asked Joey eagerly.

"Oh, a couple or three years."

"We couldn't live here that long," objected Mrs. Brown. "I'll try to hold onto the land if I can. Keep up the taxes. But my widow's pension doesn't cover food and clothes for all of us."

"There's the professor's board," said Joan. "We'll have that every summer now. And the money the museum will pay for the fossils. The professor thinks he can work through November, anyway, and he'll be back as early as he can in the spring."

"If we didn't have to buy everything we ate, we might manage," said Mrs. Brown. "But we do, so we can't."

"If you could get through this winter," said Mr. Jones thoughtfully, "you could be nearly self-supporting so far as food goes by next summer. Grow your own vegetables. Women can them, don't they? Get a cow and chickens and turkeys. Maybe a few pigs."

"We got chickens once, but the coyotes got them in one night," Joan told him. "And cows are expensive. We were going to get one, but they cost too much."

"If we had the material to work with, I think you kids and I could build a poultry house to keep out Mr. Coyote," said Mr. Jones.

"Materials cost money too," Mrs. Brown reminded him. "I can't use up our savings. Besides, gardens don't do well here. The children carried water till I thought their poor little backs would break, but they couldn't carry enough."

"I don't see why they should carry any," objected Mr. Jones. "You've got a well. Let it do the work. Put in a windmill."

"You don't understand," said Mrs. Brown. "All these things would be fine if we had the money to buy them. But we don't."

"I do," said Joey. "As soon as it comes. The reward money."

"Oh, no, Joey," said his mother. "I don't want you to pour that into this old ranch. Put it in the bank. I want

you to go to college someday."

"Let him invest it here," urged Mr. Jones. "It'll come back with interest when you finally get ready to sell. If you do sell, that is. These kids love this place, Mrs. Brown. They'll learn a lot from living here and helping to run it. There's probably a Four-H in that school in Silo. They'll learn from experts about gardening and raising animals. As the place grows, so will they. This will be wheat land as soon as you can afford to put it in. There's money in it. Big money. Joey is nuts about engines. He can run harvesters and combines and tractors to his heart's content."

"Oh, boy," said Joey, his eyes shining.

"How about me?" asked Joan.

"You'll take prizes for baking and canning," said Mr. Jones promptly. "And maybe you'll enter sheep or cows or chickens in the stock show and come home with a blue ribbon."

"I'd rather enter a horse," decided Joan thoughtfully. "I'd like to raise one. A colt, to keep Daisy Belle company."

"I'll buy you one," offered Joey promptly. "I'd rather have a car. Horses are too slow."

"Well, Mrs. Brown?" said Mr. Jones.

"Oh, dear," she sighed helplessly. "You make it sound so easy, and I know it won't be. It will be hard work for everybody. But it's Joey's money. If he really wants to spend it this way, I suppose I'll have to say yes. After all, the land is still here. Even if it doesn't work out as we hope, we can always get some of the money back. We'll stay."

After that they were busier than ever. The materials for the poultry house, like the parts for the plane, were not carried in Silo, and had to be ordered. The windmill, Mr. Jones admitted, was a little beyond him, so a carpenter had to be found to build that. Mrs. Brown decided that, with the opening of school only a few weeks away, it was high time to start making new clothes for the children, and it seemed as if they were forever being called inside to try something on.

Every evening they rushed to meet the professor's car to ask if he had yet managed to extricate the whole rib section of Eohippus from the rocks. He had heard from the museum by this time, and it was Eohippus, sure enough, but the museum had not set the price until they saw how much of the fossil was obtainable. Joey, especially, was anxious to know, and it seemed to him that it took a very long time to chisel the skeleton from the rocks.

In all this rush George was not forgotten, but they just couldn't find time to squeeze in a visit to the cliffs. One morning, however, Joan insisted that it simply could not be put off any longer.

"You know how easy it is to hurt his feelings," she reminded Joey. "He's going to think we don't like him any more."

"That's silly," said Joey. "Of course we do."

"And we owe him a lot too," insisted Joan. "When you come right down to it, we owe him everything. If it hadn't been for George, Mr. Jones wouldn't have stayed here so long, and you wouldn't have got the reward money. And Professor Harris wouldn't have Eohippus, and by this time we'd be back in town."

"I know it. You don't have to tell me," said Joey in a sulky tone. "But will Mom let us leave? She wouldn't let us go with Mr. Jones this morning, and I wanted to see how those new parts fitted in too. She said we had to stay here so we could try on clothes when she starts sewing."

At that very moment Mrs. Brown herself supplied the answer by coming to the back door.

"Children," she called. "You'll have to go up to the

rocks. The professor's forgotten his lunch. It's the first time for weeks too. He's been very careful lately."

Joan ran to get the lunch pail, and Joey to put the blanket on old Daisy Belle. Just as they were ready to ride out of the yard, a truck filled with lumber for the new windmill came down the hill.

"Maybe I ought to stay and sort of oversee," said Joey, frowning.

But Joan wouldn't let him.

"I guess they can unload without you. You're not going to build it. The carpenter is."

"But I'm building the chicken house."

"So am I," she told him smugly. Joan could hammer a nail and saw a board as straight as her brother, and she never let him forget it. "I guess it will keep till we get back. Come on. Somehow I've got a funny feeling. I think we'd better see George right away."

He clucked to Daisy Belle as soon as the truck was out of the way, and they rode slowly up the hill. It was not so warm today as it had been. When they awoke in the morning there was a distinct feel of approaching autumn in the air. There was a little haze in the sky, like a thin veil over the summer's startling blue, and in the west it gathered even thicker. There it could have been clouds or smoke from fires.

Old Daisy Belle stopped to rest in the middle of the hill, and Joan nudged her brother.

"Listen," she said. "Crickets! They came, just as the professor said they would."

Sure enough. Down in the dry creek bed came a brave

little sound, not too unlike that made by the kitchen rocker.

"You mean cricket," corrected Joey. "There's only one."

"More will come," said Joan confidently.

"If we didn't have to build a chicken house, we could find him and put him in a jar," said Joey, then immediately discarded the idea. "But that's kid stuff. We're ranchers. We've got important things to do."

They found the professor working away with his chisels and brushes. A good portion of the rib section was now clear from the rocks and protected by strips of hardened burlap. The professor didn't look so tired these days. He went around with his sunburned face beaming with enthusiasm and success.

"Just put it down," he told them. "I won't stop right now to eat it."

"But you have to eat your lunch," Joan reminded him in a tone like her mother's.

"I will, I will," he promised. "Just put it down. I'll eat it later."

He hardly looked up when they left, and certainly did not notice that Daisy Belle was not headed back to the ranch but farther up the chain of rocks.

"Even if he does see us, he won't think anything about it," said Joan comfortably. "He'll just think we're going for a little ride, and pretty soon he'll forget all about that."

"There's Mr. Jones' plane though," remembered Joey. "It's sitting out a ways from the place we always meet

George. He'll see us."

"We'll tell him we're helping the professor look for new fossils," decided Joan.

So they headed Daisy Belle away from the rocks and toward the place where the plane had come down. Mr. Jones had his head inside, close to the engine, when they arrived, but he pulled it out and spoke to them cheerfully.

"Hi. What're you two doing here?"

"The professor forgot his lunch, and we brought it to him," explained Joan quickly. "As long as we're here, we thought we might look around in those rocks up there and see if we can't find any more signs of fossils."

"Good enough." Mr. Jones nodded and went back to his repairs.

They left Daisy Belle tied in the shade cast by the plane and walked over to the rocks.

"We don't dare call," said Joan in a low voice. "Mr. Jones might hear, even this far away. And besides, with a stranger in sight, George wouldn't show himself. We'd better climb up some of these rocks and down on the other side, so we're out of sight of the plane."

They started climbing, and because they had traveled it before they found themselves on the route which led to the hot springs.

"Keep on going," urged Joey. "He just might be there. I don't think his cave is too far away from the springs."

They made the last climb, then looked down into the

little gully where George had taken them with such pride. It had changed from the times they had seen it before. The rocky ground had always been studded with holes, but today it looked as though it had been completely turned over by an excavating crew. The holes were deep, yawning pits, like foundations dug for small basements, and the soil piled high about them made them seem even deeper. Nor was there a steaming pool of scalding water in the middle. That, too, was gone.

"What's happened?" cried Joan in alarm.

"We must be in the wrong place," decided Joey.

But they weren't in the wrong place, for at that moment part of the rocky cliff below them seemed to move and then took the jagged, irregular shape of the stegosaurus.

"George!" they both cried at once, and started to clamber down the rocks so fast they were in danger of breaking their necks.

George stood quietly waiting for them. His small head hung low, and the spiked tail dragged listlessly on the ground. Even the formidable spikes along his back did not look so dangerous today.

"I was afraid you wouldn't come," he told them when they arrived breathlessly before him. "I couldn't wait any longer. I was afraid I'd have to go away without saying good-by."

"Going away? Where are you going? Why?"

"I am going because I have to. Because I am stupid."

"I never did believe you were stupid," said Joan

angrily. "It just isn't so."

"I never really believed it, either," admitted George. "That's why I kept telling people I was. So they wouldn't know I really thought I was pretty clever. My brain was small, but I always thought it had great capabilities. Now I see that I was wrong."

"But what made you change your mind all of a sudden?" demanded Joey.

"See for yourself," said George flatly. "See what I have done. I have choked up the little opening to my hidden river."

"But why?"

"It was my shyness. I heard that man who was digging for the mammal bone say that many strangers would come here. I don't want strangers here. I don't want to spend my time hiding from them."

"But George," protested Joan. "You said you could keep out of sight. You told me to show the professor that bone."

"I know I did," confessed George. "It was my fault. I alone am to blame. I didn't mind one stranger, but I certainly didn't think there would be more than one who would come looking for mammal bones."

"Oh, George," cried Joan. "I'm so sorry."

"It's my own fault," George reassured her again. "I don't blame you in the least. I told you to show it to him. It was my own stupidity. But when I realized what I had done, I didn't know what to do next. I was shivering with embarrassment. I rushed here to sharpen my tail, because that always makes me feel better. Oh, what a sharpening I gave it! When I had finished, I did feel better so I decided to have a drink. Then I discovered to my horror that I had covered up the opening to my hidden river. I'd completely choked it off and piled dirt and rocks on top of it."

"We'll find it again," said Joan. "We know it's here somewhere. Why don't you try sharpening your tail again? Maybe you'll uncover it."

"I did," confessed the stegosaurus. "I've sharpened it again and again. I've been trying to find the opening for many days. But it's gone. It won't come back."

"We'll give you water from our well," promised Joey. "We're going to have a windmill, and there'll be all the water you want."

"That kind of water is tasteless," said George sadly. "And cold besides. It's nothing to put in one's stomach. No, I must go away and find another opening in the hidden river. I don't ask for much, but I can't live without food and water."

"But maybe you can't find another. Maybe there isn't one."

"Oh, yes, there is," said George. "There's another opening to the river and plenty of sagebrush growing near by. I'll find it, never fear. There's only one thing I regret."

"What's that, George?" asked Joan quickly.

"I shall never see you two again," said the stegosaurus sadly. "And I shall know loneliness once more."

"Maybe you'll see us. Maybe we'll come where you are."

"I probably wouldn't recognize you," said George, shaking his head. "You see, everything changes, the world and everything in it. Everything but me. Good-by, little friends."

They stood openmouthed, but no words came to them. There was so much they wanted to say. They wanted to persuade him to remain, to explain how much he had done for them, and to assure him that the ranch on Cricket Creek would never be the same without him. Surely, if they all put their minds to work on the problem, they must find a solution somewhere.

But the stegosaurus didn't give them a chance to regain their breath and recover from their surprise. He turned on his huge padded feet and started up the cliff. A moment later his jagged shape had melted into the rocks.